Eddy is Back

And here he was, back again. "Eddy, what do you think you're doing? You're in a Secured Area."

"It's a barn."

"It's a barn that happens to be under tight security."

"Playing ball."

"I see that you're playing ball and that's nice. Coons need to stay busy with something."

He threw the ball up in the air and caught it. "Right. Moonlight Madness. Can't sit still, got to boogey."

I paced around him and gave him a steady gaze. He didn't seem as concerned about this deal as he should have been. After throwing the ball in the air several times, now he was rolling it around in his hands. I had to admit, he had an amazing pair of hands.

"Eddy, I've got nothing personal against you. It just happens that we're on opposite sides of the law. Coons are not allowed anywhere close to this barn. For security reasons, I can't tell you why, so you'll just have to take my word for it."

the
Red Rubber Ball

John R. Erickson

Illustrations by Nicolette G. Earley
in the style of Gerald L. Holmes

Maverick Books, Inc.

MAVERICK BOOKS, INC.
Published by Maverick Books, Inc.
P.O. Box 549, Perryton, TX 79070
Phone: 806.435.7611
www.hankthecowdog.com

First published in the United States of America by Maverick Books, Inc. 2020.

1 3 5 7 9 10 8 6 4 2

Copyright © John R. Erickson, 2020

To our bossy sons, Scot and Mark,
who have insisted we rebuild
the house we lost in the fire.

CONTENTS

CHAPTER ONE

Morning At Slim's Place

I t's me again, Hank the Cowdog. The mystery began in the fall, as I recall, on a Monday. Or was it Tuesday? Wait, it might have been Thursday.

You know what? I really don't care what day it was, and neither does anyone else. I'm telling the story and I can make it whatever day I want, and I say it was Monday.

There! A dog has to step up and take charge.

So, yes, it was a normal Monday in a normal week on the ranch. Monday followed Tuesday and Tuesday followed Wednesday, and now we're ready to get on with the business.

What were we discussing? I don't remember.

This is frustrating and it makes the Security Division look like a bunch of goofballs, dogs who

1

wake up in a new world every day and can't tell you whether it's raining or Tuesday. That might describe Drover but not me.

Wait. The weather. Now we're cooking.

Okay, Tuesday started out as one of those gorgeous days we get in the fall: soft air, not much wind, and golden light that made long shadows. The leaves on the elms and chinaberry trees had turned yellow, and the wild plums and skunkbrush added splashes of bright red to the overall so-forth. In other words, we had us a beautiful autumn day on the ranch, the kind of day that dogs and people would like to hang onto for a long time.

Drover and I had spent the night at Slim's place, down the creek and two miles east of headquarters. As usual, I flew out of bed before first light and was ready to go out and face the new day. Drover remained conked out on the living room floor, sleeping his life away.

I found Slim in the kitchen, slurping on his first cup of coffee and cooking breakfast. That's a joke, by the way, "cooking breakfast." He's a bachelor and doesn't cook anything for breakfast. He boils his coffee in a pan, and if he eats breakfast, it comes out of a can or a box... although once in a while, he'll eat a left-over boiled turkey neck.

Have you ever looked at a cold, boiled turkey neck first thing in the morning? Gag.

But, most usually, if he eats breakfast, it comes out of a box or a can, and on this particular morning, a Thursday, as I recall, it came out of a box of Roastie Toasties. That's a brand of cereal, don't you see. He dumped some flakes into a bowl and added a splash of milk.

You'll be proud to know that I was right there at his feet, cheering him on to a good, nourishing breakfast and...well, hoping he might share some of it. Not a lot, just a few morsels. I mean, dogs need nourishment too.

I moved my front paws up and down and scootched a little closer.

He shoveled the first bite of Toasties into his mouth and crunched them up. His soggy eyes popped open and the spoon froze in mid-air. "Huh. That milk's a little blinky."

Blinky? Never heard of it.

He gazed into the bowl. "And what are those things?" He looked closer. "They're swimming around. You want to finish this, pooch?"

What? Yes, of course! What an amazing piece of good luck.

He set the bowl on the floor in front of me and

I flipped all the switches for the Obedient Dog Program. It's a silly little ritual, and we have to play along with it. We have to sit like perfect doggies until he gives us permission to eat. I told you it was silly.

Tensing every muscle in my highly-conditioned body, I looked up at him and waited for his command. He lifted his right hand. I leaned toward the bowl.

"Not yet."

Fine. I could wait.

"Hank, we need to start with our Thought For the Day."

Could we get on with this?

"Here it is. Pay attention."

Oh brother.

"See no weevil, eat no weevil." His hand swept downward and pointed toward the bowl. "Go for it!"

I hit the Launch button and began lapping milk and...you know, it had an odd taste, the milk did, kind of...not terrible, but not so great either. No problem. I plunged on with the procedure and thirty seconds later, I had devoured the cereal, lapped the milk, licked the bowl, and was giving him our look that says, "Is that all?"

He wasn't watching because he had opened a

can of jalapeno bean dip and was eating it with a
spoon. Breakfast.

It smelled pretty yummy, so I lit up the
"Starving" sign in my eyes and began sweeping

the floor with my tail. He shook his head. "That's all you get, and it's more than you deserve. How were the weevils?"

Weevils? The cereal had been okay, but the milk...you know, it had left a bad taste in my mouth. I had ignored it during the Eating Experience, but now...well, it lingered and I noticed a sourish taste.

And suddenly I understood the meaning of "blinky." *The carton of milk had been in his ice box so long, it had gone bad!* But instead of throwing it out or feeding it to an ungrateful cat, he had dumped it off on his loyal friend—ME!

You know, a ranch dog can never relax or let down his guard. If we're not being attacked by Charlie Monsters, we're being fed tainted food by our so-called "friends."

Oh well, we take what we can get for breakfast. Now...what about that bean dip?

Too late. He had hogged it all. "Let's go to work, pooch. The boss'll be pacing the floor till we get there."

Rats.

I left the kitchen with a heavy heart and turned to the task of rooting Drover out of bed. As you might have guessed, he was still curled up in a little white ball in the middle of the living room floor. Filling my air tanks as I went, I marched over to him and leaned down until my nose almost touched his left ear.

Once in position, I activated "Train Horns," a barking procedure that has a wondrous effect on sleeping slackers. BWONK! Heh, heh. Mister Squeak and Grunt sprang two feet in the air and appeared to be trying to swim.

"Help, murder, skiffer pork chopping the gingerbread cottage!"

He crashed back to the floor and stared at me with wide eyes that expressed...well, not much. No kidding, we're talking about Lights On But Nobody Home. In other words, I was getting a glimpse into the emptiness of his Inner Bean.

Wait, hold everything. "Inner Bean" and "bean dip." Was this some kind of clue that needed to be checked out? I studied on it for a few seconds, then...nah, nothing there.

Anyway, Drover stared at me and said, "Oh my gosh, I heard a terrible noise!"

"You heard me. I did Train Horns to wake you up."

"You were training the corn to wake me up?" He glanced around and blinked his eyes. "Where's the corn?"

"There is no corn."

"Then where did all the cornbread come from?"

I knew this was just a trickle of gibberish, leaking out of his sleeping mind, but I was curious to see where it might lead. Sometimes our best clues come from strange sources, don't you know, so I began my interrogation. "What cornbread are we talking about?"

"Well, there was this gingerbread house."

"You said it was a cottage."

"No, there was some cottage cheese."

"All right, go on."

"The house was made of cornbread."

"Whoa, stop right there. A gingerbread house can't be made of cornbread."

"How come?"

"Because it would go against the Laws of Figgy. A brick house is made of bricks. A gingerbread house must be made of gingerbread. A house made of cornbread would be a *cornbread* house."

"I'll be derned. Well, it was cuttered with buvver."

"Hold it. Do you mean it was 'covered with butter'?"

"Yeah, did you eat some?"

"No."

His gaze swept around the room. "Somebody

8

did. It must have been the frog."

"What frog?"

"Well, there was this frog."

"I need details, Drover, a description. What did he look like?"

"Well, he was ugly and had a big frog mouth."

"All frogs have a big frog mouth."

"What about little frogs?"

"A little frog has a *little* big frog mouth. Was the frog little or big?"

"Well...he was big enough so that his feet touched the ground."

"Now we're getting somewhere. So you think this frog ate the cornbread house that was covered with butter?"

"No, it was a gingerbread house."

I roasted him with a glare. "Drover, it was a cornbread house. We've already covered this."

He twisted his head to the side and gave me a puzzled look. "Who'd want to make a house out of cornbread?"

"I don't know. This was all your invention. I'm just trying to...I don't know what I'm trying to do."

Just then, Slim's voice boomed. "Come on, dogs, load up, we're burning daylight!"

Drover glanced around and lowered his voice. "See? He said, 'Come on, frogs.' He's calling the frogs."

What a waste of time. I stuck my nose in his face and gave him a growl. "He said 'dogs,' not 'frogs.' Wake up, soldier, and return to base."

He blinked his eyes. "Gosh, was I asleep?"

"I hope so, because if you weren't asleep, you're crazier than a bedbug. Let's move out."

And that's how my Wednesday got started, listening to Drover's nonsense. But just then... you'll never guess what happened.

CHAPTER TWO

A Raccoon Crosses
the Road (Major Clue)

Well, my interrogation proved to be a waste of time, but in my line of work, we have to follow every lead and clue, even the ones that seem pointless. Sometimes a pointless clue will point the case in an entirely new direction, but this time...

Let's disregard the interrogation, just wad up the transcript and pitch it into the trash. All we need to take from this experience is that *Drover is a weird little mutt.*

Back to business. As we were leaving the house, the telephone rang.

In some parts of the world, the ringing of a phone is no big deal and nothing out of the ordinary. At Slim's place, it was unusual because... well, who would call a bachelor cowboy who lived twenty-fives miles out in the country?

Yet somebody was calling. Slim was halfway out the door and I heard him grumble, "Why can't people just leave me alone? I'm going to have that thing disconnected. Get out of the way, dog."

He stumbled over me (was that my fault?) and snatched up the phone. "Hello. Yes. Well, I'm tripping over dogs and trying to get some work done. Who is this? Oh. Well, I'll get there as quick as I can. No, I won't hurry. I'll drive my usual speed and I'll get there when I get there. I'd already be there if people would quit calling me on the dadgum phone. Bye."

He hung up the phone and looked down at me. "Loper. He's got ants in his pants and needed to bother someone. I never should have given him my phone number...course, he's the one who pays the bill. Let's go."

Aye, aye, sir! Back to work.

Slim went to the door and held it open for us. "Hurry up, I don't have all day to wait on a couple of soup hounds. Y'all make termites look like Olympic sprinters."

He loves to go on like this, blustering and complaining about the dogs, and blaming us for things we didn't do...such as termites. Was it our fault that termites spent all their time running races? No, but you'll notice who borp, excuse me, got blamed for it. The dogs.

And while we're on the subject of indigestion, let me point out that no dog in history was ever enough of a scrounge to give his friend A BOWL OF SPOILED MILK, but that's exactly what Slim had done to me. He had forced me to consume a bowl of poisoned milk laced with...

Remember those "weevils" he mentioned? At the time, the word didn't register on my registration, but after a few minutes of thought, the true meaning of the word had come into focus.

A weevil is a BUG. Slim saw bugs in his cereal, I mean, they were swimming laps around the bowl, and he didn't want to eat a bunch of bugs. So what did he do? He gave it to his trusted friend, his loyal bupp, excuse me, his loyal dog and forced me to swill it down like a common hog.

What an outrage! Is this what we've come to, you can't trust cowboys any more? Let down your guard for one minute and they'll feed you bugs and poisoned milk?

It's a sad state of affairs, that's all I'll say.

Okay, there might be one more question. Why do I keep eating the garbage he puts in front of me? That's a toughie and we're out of time. Sorry.

Actually, spoiled milk isn't as bad as you

might suppose and it beats nothing. What's a dog supposed to do, eat a bowl of air for breakfast? And I'll tell you something else. Some experts on nutrition have demonstrated that a few bugs in your Toasties isn't such a bad deal. Weevils are a form of meat, don't forget, and they increase the protein level of the ork, excuse me.

So there you are. Don't make snap judgments about dogs and what we eat. We're just trying to make a living. Furthermore, that little spell of indigestion had passed, further proof that a determined, red-blooded American dog can digest anything that doesn't digest him first.

Sorry, I didn't mean to get carried away, but this gives you a glimpse at the kind of issues a Head of Ranch Security has to deal with in an average day. We're talking about MAJOR ISSUES, hundreds of them. Ordinary mutts are free to goof off and live careless lives, but those of us on Life's High Ground must carry a heavy load.

Wait. Should we do a song about this? Maybe so, because I just thought of one. Here, listen to this.

We Have Bugs

We have bugs in the cereal and bugs in the bowl.
I have bugs in my belfry and weevils in my soul.
They are frolicking like porpoises and swimming

14

down my back.

They are playing water polo in my alimentary tract.

The data suggest we have bugs.
The evidence is clear, we have bugs.
We have bugs.

What do you think? It was kind of a simple song, but it had a powerful message about all the so-forths of Life In the Real World, and any time a dog can dress up Ordinary Experience in the finery of melody and song, by George, he should do it.

Now...where were we? Oh yes, it was a lovely, soft autumn morning when we loaded up in Slim's pickup and drove west on the county road. As usual, I took my position beside the shotgun-side window.

As usual, Drover started whining. "Can I ride Shotgun?"

"Absolutely not, and do you know why? Because you led me into a ridiculous conversation about cornbread houses and frogs."

"Well, you woke me up and made me answer a bunch questions."

"Asking questions is part of my job."

"You never let me ride Shotgun."

I heaved a sigh. "Drover, what would you do if I let you ride Shotgun? Would it change your life even a tiny bit?"

"Well, I could stick my head out the window and breathe fresh air."

"What's wrong with the air you're breathing now?"

"It smells like dogs."

"What did you expect? When dogs are riding in a pickup, the air should *smell* like dogs—honest, hard-working ranch dogs."

"Yeah, but it stinks."

"Had you thought of taking a bath?"

"I hate water."

"You have too many problems. I can't help you." I turned my back on the runt.

"You could let me ride Shotgun."

I whirled around and glared at him. "You really think that would make you happy?" He grinned and bobbed his head. "All right, I guess you're old enough to give it a shot."

"No fooling?"

"But if it doesn't bring you Happiness and Bliss, I don't want to hear you complaining about it. Can you handle that?"

He was almost beside himself. "Oh yeah, this'll be great!"

We traded spots and I gave him a few minutes to settle into his new position. "Well? Is your life any better?"

"No."

"What's the problem?"

"The window's rolled up and the air stinks over here too."

"Well, I don't know what to say."

"Can I have my old place back?"

"No, sorry. I've decided that I like it here in the middle."

"I miss my old spot. Please?"

"Oh, all right." We traded places. "There. Are you happy now?"

"I don't know. I'm all confused."

"But did you learn anything from this experience?"

"Yeah, you cheat."

"Drover, it's not my fault that the window was rolled up."

"Yeah, but you could have told me." His lip quivered. "I never dreamed you'd turn into a cheater-cheater-rotten-egg-eater."

I laid a paw upon his shoulder. "Son, there's a very important lesson here, so pay attention. *The grass is always greener when the grass greens up.*"

"I don't get it."

"Brown grass never looks as green as green grass, because brown grass has a brownish color."

"Gosh, I never thought of that." His eyes brightened and he beamed a silly grin. "Does it mean that I'm happier than I thought?"

"Yes."

"I'm not depressed any more?"

"That's correct, and you didn't even have to eat grass."

"Gosh, thanks. I feel a whole lot better now."

"Good, good. Now sit back and enjoy the ride."

You know, a lot of dogs in my position wouldn't have taken the time to coach their employees through difficult times, but me? I considered it part of my job. See, I knew that deep down inside, Drover *wanted* to ride in the middle of the seat, but he needed a friend to guide him to the right conclusion.

Pretty touching, huh? You bet. Drover seemed as chirpy as a little sparrow, now that he was right back where he'd started in the first place.

Weird.

We made the rest of the trip without any problems...wait, there was one small incident. As we were chugging along, Slim hit the brakes to avoid hitting a raccoon that was crossing the road.

"Good honk, that coon's got a red ball in his mouth! Now, that's one for the record book. And he kind of looks like Eddy."

I admit that I didn't see the coon or the so-called red ball, because I was trying to scratch an itch on my nose. It's a very delicate procedure that requires concentration and a soft touch with a hind foot. See, if you bear down too hard with the Scratcher, you can put a big hurt on your nose.

So, yes, I was distracted, didn't witness the coon with my own eyes, and didn't give it another thought until hours later. By that time...well, you'll see. It turned out to be a major clue in a case that hasn't yet begun to begin.

CHAPTER THREE

A Town Mutt Shows Up on the Ranch

When we reached headquarters, we saw Loper coming out of the house. He walked over to Slim's window. "Afternoon."

"Loper, it's morning and I got here as quick as I could."

"Morning."

"Does that mean 'good morning?' Or 'Good morning, Slimbo, it's great to see you again'?"

"It was a simple statement of fact. It's morning and there's nothing I can do about it."

"Yeah, but are you thrilled to see me?"

"Not yet."

"Come on now, dig a little deeper. Don't seeing me first thing in the morning make everything seem just a little brighter?"

Loper gave him a blank stare. "What's wrong with you? Have you been drinking mouthwash?"

"Loper, I'm just trying to spread a little sunshine to make up for your warped personality."

"The nice thing about a radio is that you can change stations."

"You need to lighten up and be thankful for little blessings."

"If you find one, let me know."

"Well, I've got one. Listen to this. I found weevils in my breakfast food this morning, and almost ate 'em."

"And that's a blessing?"

Slim reached across the cab and gave me a pat on the head. "Hankie stepped in and saved me. He ate every bug. John Wayne never did anything that brave."

Loper finally surrendered to a chuckle. "Okay, our dog's a hero. That's something to celebrate."

Wow, did you hear that? Me, a hero! I was amazed. I mean, it was true, of course, but on this outfit, a dog can wait years for that kind of recognition. I sat up straight and thrashed my tail against the seat. This was a very proud...

They weren't even looking me. Boy, you've got to grab your glory fast, while it's there, because it doesn't last long.

Loper's smile had faded and his face had returned to its earlier, frozen state. "We've got ten tons of cottonseed cake headed this way."

"I thought they were bringing it tomorrow."

"They're bringing it today and he'll be here any time. The truck driver won't be bringing an extra hand. His helper called in sick."

Slim stretched out his arms and yawned. "No problem. A couple of big strapping lads like me and you won't have any trouble with ten tons of cake."

Loper looked at his wristwatch. "I've got a meeting with the accountant and need to get moving." He smirked and gave Slim a pat on the arm. "Take your time, drink plenty of water, and don't wear yourself out."

Slim beamed him a glare. "Loper, you're a skunk, that's all I can say."

"I know, I hate it." He winked and headed for the house. "Be happy in your work."

Slim turned to me. "He's a skunk and this is a put-up deal. One of these days, the hired hands are going to rise up and protest the injustice of this world." I guess he was talking to me but, well, I happened to be in the middle of a yawn. "Hey, pay attention! Injustice rules the land and all you can do is yawn about it."

Well, excuse me! Was it my fault that Loper

was a skunk? And for his information, dogs need to yawn once in a while.

Gee, what a grouch.

We drove around to the cake house, which sat on a piece of flat ground northwest of the machine shed. Actually, it was an old one-room school house that Loper had moved to headquarters years ago, and that's where we stored our winter's supply of cake.

By the way, we're not talking about birthday cake. It was "cow cake" made of cottonseed meal, also known as "pelleted feed." It's kind of amazing that a dog would know so much about this stuff, isn't it? You bet.

A truck was backing up to the door when we got there. The driver set his brakes, shut off the motor, and climbed out of the cab. He wore striped overalls and an old felt hat, and he'd brought his dog, a homely mutt named Roy. He had a bob tail and a patch of black over one eye—Roy did, not the driver—and might have been part-Australian shepherd—again, the dog not the driver.

Most of your Aussies are okay. They do good work and mind their own business, but this guy...I don't know, there was a cocky air about him, and a shifty look. After you've been in the Security Business for a while, you can pick 'em out. They think they're just a little bit better than the rest of us, and it usually leads to trouble.

Whilst the men went to work unloading fifty-pound sacks of feed, I kept a close watch on Roy. Sure enough, he went to the southwest corner of the cake house and lifted his leg. (What did I tell you?)

"Hey, you! No marks on my barn."

He dropped his leg. "I've been in that truck for a long time."

"That's not my problem. Go find a weed."

"Well, whatever you think." He went to a clump of ragweed and sniffed it. "How about this one?"

"No, that's a special weed. Go out in the pasture."

He shot me a sour look and trotted out in the pasture until he came to a clump of yucca. "This be okay?"

"No, that's special too. Keep going." He moved farther north until he came to a clump of broom weed. "That'll work, go for it."

Maybe I shouldn't have been so fussy—I mean, let's be honest, I didn't care about the weeds—but a guy has to be firm when town dogs show up on his ranch.

When Roy returned from his mission, I went straight to the southwest corner of the cake house and laid down a good, strong mark. "This is MY barn, so don't get any big ideas. And by the way, I'm Head of Ranch Security."

He shrugged. "Fair enough...but don't be messing with the tires on my truck."

My ears shot up. "What did you say?"

"That's my truck. I ride Shotgun."

"And that's a big deal?"

"Yep, big deal. Guess who barks at every car we pass. Me. And cattle trucks get a double shot."

We glared at each other for several seconds and things got pretty tense. Then I decided to defuse the situation.

"Let's move on to something else. This seems a little childish."

"I agree. Plumb silly, in fact."

I stepped away from him. "Sometimes we take ourselves too seriously."

"I guess we do. Dogs are funny." We shared a little laugh. "But you have to admit that riding Shotgun in a big old Peterbilt is about as awesome as it gets."

"Why do I have to admit that?"

"Well, because it's true. I mean, you might think that riding around in a ranch pickup is hot stuff, but that's only because you don't have a real truck."

"Ha! That truck of yours is a piece of junk."

"Yeah? It's ten times better than that pile-of-junk barn of yours."

Again, we glared and bristled, then I paced a few steps away. "You know what? This is a ridiculous conversation."

"I agree."

"Let's end it here."

"Done. All I'm saying is, *that's my truck*."

"Fine, it's your truck."

I thought that would put an end to the nonsense, but he just had to keep running his big mouth. "And don't be messing with my tires."

I felt the hair rising on the back of my neck. "I couldn't care less about your tires, but let me point out that your truck is parked on MY ranch."

"Hey, George, you got it backwards. Your ranch is parked under MY truck, so maybe you ought to move your ranch."

We began circling each other. "Did you call me 'George'?"

"I sure did, and I'll call you George any time I want."

"I'd advise you not to do that."

"George, George, George!"

Well, that did it. The mutt had crossed the line, calling me George, and I was ready to go into some heavy combat. I stuck my nose in his flanks and he stuck his nose in mine. We bristled and made teeth at each other. We circled and growled and snarled, and I was just about ready to clean his plow, when a voice ripped through the tensionous air.

"Hank, knock it off!"

Huh? Okay, Slim and the driver had stopped for a water break. They were standing outside the cake house and...well, watching us, it appeared. Slim yelled, "Come here!" I went to Slim and The Mouth went to his guy. Slim said, "Hank, what's the problem?"

Well, I...we...he called me George.

The truck driver said, "Roy, what's the problem?"

Roy gave him a dumb look and tapped his tail. He seemed to be saying, "It's my truck."

The men exchanged glances and shook their heads, and Slim said, "Bird brains. Y'all be nice. If you can't think of anything better," he swatted at a yellow jacket wasp, "you might do something about these frazzling wasps."

They took another drink of water and went back to work, lugging bags of feed into the barn and putting them into stacks. Roy and I were left alone and, well, it was kind of awkward—two old enemies left alone on the field of battle.

I slid a glance his direction and he did the same to me. He wagged his tail three times and

I answered back. We seemed to be moving toward a peaceful solution to the crisis and someone needed to step up and show some maturity, so I

said, "Okay, I'll admit it's your truck."

"Thanks."

"And it's nice truck, not a piece of junk."

"Thanks, bud, that means a lot. It's the best truck I've ever owned and I'm proud of it." The expression on his face softened. "Hey, I'm sorry I called you George."

"Thanks. It was nothing, really. I shouldn't be so touchy about little things."

"Right. I guess we both need to work on that."

"I agree. What matters is that we share the Brotherhood of All Dogs."

"You got it. Hey, without us dogs, where would the world be?"

"Exactly. The world would be a complete mess." There was a long moment of silence. "Well, what shall we do now?"

He shrugged. "Beats me. Seems kind of boring, don't it?" Then his face brightened. "Hey, I've got an idea, and this'll be fun."

Hmm. I wondered what he had in mind for our "fun."

I Give Roy
Some Schooling

R oy stood up, stretched, and shook the grass off his coat. He pointed a paw toward several wasps that were buzzing above our heads. A grin tugged at the corners of his mouth. "You see all those bugs?"

"Yes, they're called 'yellow jackets,' and they're a variety of wasp. At this time of year, they come out of wherever they spent the summer and the air is filled with them. They land on every surface and become a nuisance. What else would you like to know about wasps?"

He gave me a blank stare. "Well, I wasn't asking about 'em. I think I know quite a bit about wasps."

"Roy, you might know a few facts about wasps

in general, but these particular wasps are on my ranch."

"A wasp is a wasp."

"A wasp is a wasp, but nobody knows more about the wasps on my ranch than I do. If that hurts your feelings, I'm sorry, but I must remind you that I'm Head of Ranch Security."

He rolled his eyes. "Yeah, I think you mentioned that." He moved a step closer. "Listen, bud, I'm in charge of a feed warehouse in town, huge. It makes that barn of yours look like a chicken house, and we've got a billion yellow jackets."

"Yes, and that's my whole point. There are two kinds of wasp in this world: yours and mine. You might know a few things about *your* wasps, but you don't know beans about mine."

He shook his head and looked away. "Boy, talking to you is like talking to a pallet of salt blocks."

"All you have to do is admit that I know more about my wasps than you do."

He heaved a sigh. "Okay. We'll agree on that."

"See? That wasn't so bad."

He beamed a grin. "Now, do you know how to catch one?"

"Well, I...why would I want to catch a wasp?"

"Insect control. I do it all the time at the warehouse. Part of my job. Y'all don't do that out here?"

"I didn't say that. Of course we do, but...well, our wasps sting."

He laughed. "They all do, son. You've got to know the right technique. Watch this."

He walked toward the cake house and as he walked, his eyes swept the airspace in front of him, which contained five or six buzzing yellow jackets. He stopped and studied them.

To be honest, I found this a little boring, so I said, "Uh...Roy, let me suggest..."

"Shhh. I can't concentrate with you flapping your mouth. We're getting close to something. Steady...steady..."

When one of the wasps landed on the ground near the door, he moved forward in a rapid walk, seized the wasp in his mouth, clicked his teeth five times, and gave his head a vigorous shake. The wasp flew out of his mouth and landed on the ground.

He turned to me with a grin. "Dead bug. What do you think?"

"Well, it was okay, not bad, I mean, we do it all the time out here."

"Let's see how you do it."

"Me? With a live wasp?"

He chuckled and shook his head. "You can't kill a dead one."

"I'm aware of that, Roy, but...actually, I wouldn't mind watching you do it one more time."

"Ten-four on that."

I wasn't sure exactly what the mutt was trying to pull, but I was pretty sure that I had just witnessed a demonstration of Dumb Luck. Hey, I'd had plenty of experience with yellow jackets and knew what they can do. They sting and it hurts like crazy. What kind of moron would put one into his mouth?

Roy swept his gaze across the air above his head and seemed to lock on one wasp in particular. He moved forward, two cautious steps. The wasp hung in the air about three feet above the ground.

In a soft voice, he said, "This 'un will be a surface-to-air deal. It can be tricky, so watch close."

"I'd appreciate it if you wouldn't..."

"Shhhh."

He stopped, froze, went into a crouch, and sprang at the wasp, snagged it out of the air, clicked his teeth, shook his head, and flipped the wasp out of his mouth.

He puffed himself up into a ridiculous pose. "Dead bug. What do you say now?"

"That wasn't bad, but it's basically the same procedure we use out here."

"The trick is to keep him in the front of your

mouth, see, and click your teeth real fast, and, don't let him..."

I cut him off with a raised paw. "Roy, I know you're trying to help, but I can handle it. Please step aside and study your lessons."

"Roger that."

He stepped out of the way and I switched on Visual Radar. I could have chosen a wasp that was on the ground, but Mister Smarty Guy had raised the level of competition by shooting one out of the air. I would have to answer the challenge by shooting not just one wasp out of the sky, but five or six.

Vizrad zoomed in on a target. He was floating in the air at exactly oh-five-three-seven degrees of multitude. I locked him into the computer and got the Go Light, sprang upward, launched the weapon and blasted him right out of the...

AAAAAAA-EEEEEE!

I hit the ground with a thud and began flinging my head around and spitting. *The stupid wasp had drilled me right in the middle of my tongue!*

Through watering eyes, I saw Smart Guy cackling and shaking his head. "Nope, nope, nope. Bad technique. You let him get too deep in your mouth. You've got to chop him up with your front teeth."

I gave him a withering glare and shoved him aside. "Get out of my way. That was just a sucker punch."

Well, the pressure was on. This time, instead of attempting a difficult surface-to-air procedure, where the wasp had a clear advantage, I picked a target that was lounging on the ground in front of the barn. Easy money, and this bug was fixing to pay a terrible price. This was war!

I breezed through the Check List (Approach, Switch On Vizrad, Lock and Load), and went thundering into combat. The wasp never knew what hit him, never had a chance to pull any cheap tricks or take evasive action. I nailed the little heathen and...

AAAAAAAA-EEEEEE!

Never mind, nothing happened. I crunched the hateful thing into a thousand pieces, spit him to the ends of the earth, and that was the end of it. Okay, something happened but I'm not going to talk about it.

Look, you don't need to know everything that goes on around here. Some of the things we do on this ranch are not open to the general public, sorry.

Phooey. I might as well come clean. You might have already guessed it anyway. I crunched the little monster into smithereens, but somehow, against incredible odds, he managed to plunge his harpoon into my lower lip—not just once, but three times! It stung so badly, my eyes almost bugged out of their sprockets. We're talking about Big Hurt.

When the water cleared from my eyes, I saw Roy laughing and shaking his head. "I ain't believing this. You done it again! Ha!"

I marched over to him and stuck my nose in his face. "Wisten, bubby, you and I are fissing to go to waw."

That brought another screech of laughter. In fact, he laughed so hard he staggered several steps, fell over, and started kicking his legs. It was then that I began to realize that...uh...the wasp stings had caused swelling to my lips and tongue and...well, it was affecting my ability to communicate.

Which was fine, because I had nothing more to say to this...this arrogant, over-bearing, smart-mouth town dog who rode around in a rattle-trap feed truck and had nothing better to do with his life than to snap at bugs. What kind of bonehead would...

Behind me, I heard another outburst of laughter, and it wasn't coming from Roy. I whirled around and saw...oh great. The men had stopped work and witnessed the whole shabby affair, and I knew what was coming.

Sure enough, Slim chuckled and shook his head. "You have to wonder what goes through a dog's mind that makes him want to put a yellow jacket wasp into his mouth."

The other guy nodded. "Yeah, but you know,

old Roy does it all the time, chews 'em up and spits 'em out, and he never seems to get stung."

"Huh. I guess Bozo skipped school the day they covered that, 'cause he definitely got drilled. Hank, if you bite a wasp, he'll bite you back. Find something else to do."

Oh brother. You see what I have to put up with around here?

I lifted my head to a proud angle and marched away from this shameless exhibition of mutter mumble, and left the small minds to mock and laugh and make fun. The mockery of small minds has never bothered me in the least.

Okay, it bothered me enough so that I wanted to be alone, so I crept around to the back side of the cake house. There, in privacy and silence, I listened to the pulse pounding inside my mouth, and we're talking about a whole concert of drums. That yellow jacket poison will turn your life around, let me tell you.

After a while, I heard the truck motor start up and knew the men had finished unloading the feed. I had recovered enough from the wasp attacks so that I could function, and marched around to the front of the barn, just as Roy was about to jump into the cab.

I yelled, "If I evoo kitch you on diss wanch again,

they'll have to take you home in a papoo thack!"

He turned and gave me exactly the kind of smirk you'd expect, and called out, "Thanks, I had a great time. You're a real piece of work, George. See you around." With one last burst of childish laughter, he leaped into the cab.

Maybe you think that was the end of it, with the mutt delivering the last shot and calling me "George." Well, you have no idea what happened next, so you'd better keep reading.

Don't forget: The mind of a dog is an awesome thing.

Drover Becomes a Smarty Pants

O kay, there we were in front of the cake house. Roy, the mutt from town, hopped into the cab of the truck. Trembling with righteous anger, I waited until the driver had climbed inside and slammed the door, then I rushed forward, hiked up my hind leg, and delivered a devastating load of Secret Corrosive Fluid to the tires.

When they pulled away from the barn, the Wasp King was grinning at me through the side window. Ha. He wouldn't be grinning for long. Little did he know that within thirty minutes, the tandem axles would MELT and DISINTEGRATE into smoking rubble, leaving him and his driver-pal stranded on the side of the highway, begging for someone to pick them up and carry them back to their fleabag warehouse in Twitchell.

Never forget: The mind of a dog is...I've already said that.

Wow, what a blow! You know, there are weapons in our arsenal that we hate to use, but some dogs just have no class or manners and have to be taught lessons the hard way.

The important thing is that I had gotten the mutt off my ranch and had turned a bitter experience into a huge moral victory, and at that point, I trotted over to the barn and went inside. There, I found Slim sweeping the floor and tidying things up. That in itself was something to remember, Slim Chance using a broom.

I walked around, inspecting the stacks of feed. The men had actually done a pretty good job of stacking. Slim was such a goof-off, you could never be sure how things might turn out, but I had to admit that the stacks looked solid and tight.

I was about to leave, when I realized that Drover had appeared out of the vapors and was standing in the doorway. Where had he been for the past two hours? We never know. Maybe he'd been hiding in the machine shed until the work was done, or he might have been fraternizing with the local cat.

I was about to scold him for leaving the job site, when I noticed...hmm, half a dozen yellow jacket wasps buzzing around. And Drover was watching them with dreamy eyes. I eased over to him.

"Dwovoo, have you evoo twied to catch a wathp?"

His gaze drifted down to me. "Oh, hi. Did you just get here?"

"Mo, I have been here foe hours. Where haff you been?"

"Well, let me think. I'm not sure, but I had a blast. I'll never forget it." He stared at me. "Gosh, your face looks different."

"I've always had a diffwent faith."

"I'll be derned. And you're talking kind of funny too."

"I'm not talking fummy. Answoo my question."

"Well, I don't remember the question."

"Have you evoo twied to catch a wathp?"

"A what?"

"A wathp, a yeah-woe jacket wathp."

"Oh. A wasp? Well, let me think here." He rolled his eyes around. "Yeah, and I was pretty good at it, too."

"Oh weally? How would you wike to put on a wittle demonstwashion?"

"A what?"

"A demonstwashion."

"A what?"

I moved closer to his ear. "A DEMONSTWA-
-SHION! What's wong wiff you?"

"Well, you don't need to scream."

"I didn't skweam. You nevoo wisten. I want
to see a demonstwashion."

"Me, catch a wasp? Oh, I'd rather not.
Sometimes they sting."

"I'm aware that thometimes they thting. Show
me how to do it, and that is a diweckt order."

"Is there a prize?"

"Yeth, there is a pwithe."

"Oh goodie. Boy, I love prizes. Here I go!"

You probably think it was mean of me to pull
this trick on the runt, and...all right, maybe it
was, but don't forget, I'd had a bad morning:
blinky milk, weevils in the cereal, indigestion,
and then, to top it off, getting bombed in the
mouth by thirty-five yellow jackets wasps.

So yes, I'd had a bad morning.

But did that give me the right to lure poor,
trusting Drover into a dirty trick? Probably not.
In fact, NO. It was a rotten thing for a dog to do,
and suddenly I was overwhelmed by a wave of
guilt. I tried to call him back, but it was too late.

He had already pounced on one of the insects and was about to put it into his mouth.

I felt like a scrounge and began preparing the text for a Complete Apology. I waited for his screams to fill the...

I couldn't believe it. The runt pounced on the wasp, clicked his teeth, shook his head, and flung it out of his mouth. Then he beamed a look of triumph and came hopping over to me. "There! What did you think of that?"

"Dwovoo, how did you do that wiffout getting thtung?"

"Oh, it wasn't a big deal, just a little trick."

"What was the twick?"

"Easy. You chop him up with your front teeth, see, before he gets a chance to use his stinger." He gave me a wink and a silly grin.

"And exakwee where did you wurn diss twick?"

He rolled his eyes around. "Oh, it's just common sense. Anyone could figure it out. Get the wasp before he gets you. Hee hee. Are you proud of me?"

To be honest, I didn't know whether I was proud of him or not. I mean, if "everybody" knew that trick, how come nobody had told ME about it?

It really burned me up, but I had no choice but to give him his prize: First Dibs on evening scraps. And that's all I want to say about it.

No, I'll say one more thing. Just when you think Drover is totally unconscious, he comes up with something that makes you think he might be partially awake. Had he spied on me and Roy? How else could you explain...

He must have cheated, but I never figured out how he did it. Phooey.

Slim finished sweeping the floor and the three of us stepped outside. He closed the door and secured it by slipping a rusted bolt into the hasp. He wiped drops of sweat off his forehead and took a deep breath of air.

"There, by grabs, the winter feed is in the barn." His gaze drifted down to the bottom of the door, where two of the boards were rotted and warped. "We need to fix that door one of these days. I sure hope the coons..." His gaze landed on me. "Hank, I don't want any coons in the barn, you got that?"

Huh? Me?

"You dogs stay here tonight and try to perform above your IQ. No coons in the cake house."

Yes sir.

But let me hasten to point out that if anyone on the ranch had asked my opinion on this, I would have offered a simple solution. FIX THE DOOR.

Here, look at this check list on how to fix a door:

- Go to the lumber yard and buy fresh wood.
- Measure the boards, make square cuts, and nail them in place.
- Or even better, use wood screws—shiny new hardware, not the rusted junk they kept in coffee cans in the machine shed.
- When the door is fixed, coons can't slither inside.
- Duh.

But does anyone around here listen to me? Oh no. They're always "covered up with work," rushing from one crisis to another, too busy to make the trip into town and do a proper job of fixing anything, so they dump it on the dogs.

Oh well, we ride for the brand and try to do our jobs. It appeared that Coon Patrol had just become Priority One for the Security Division, and we dared not fail.

Slim climbed into the pickup and drove down to the corrals to start his morning chores, putting out feed for the horses and weaning calves and doctoring a couple of sick steers that had come off a field of hay grazer.

He didn't invite us to ride in the pickup with him and that was fine with me. I had four legs and knew how to use them. Dogs that ride around all the time in a pickup become soft and pampered, and that's not me.

As we hiked back to the house, I noticed that Drover kept shooting glances in my direction, and finally I called him on it. "Why do you keep gwancing at me?"

"Oh, nothing. You've got a fat lip."

"I do not have a fat wip."

"Well, it looks fat to me."

"Has it evoo okudd to you that you might need gwasses?"

"Need what?"

"Gwasses."

"Grasses?"

"Gwasses!"

"Classes?"

I stopped, stuck my nose in his face, and screamed, "GWASSES! It is so fwustwating, twying to cawwee on a conversation wiff you, because you nevoo pay attention!"

I was stunned when the runt...well, burst out laughing. "Hee hee! I just figured it out." He was laughing so hard, he could hardly walk. "You tried to catch a wasp and got stung, and that's why you can't talk straight, hee hee! Go ahead and admit it."

For a long moment of heartbeats, I glared ice

picks at the little goof and considered the List of Drastic Measures. I ached to give him the tongue-lashing he so richly deserved but...well, my tongue had turned into a piece of sausage and was pretty muchly out of the lashing business, so I ended up giving him the worst punishment I could think of.

I marched away and left him alone with his own boring self. There! That would teach him a lesson he would never remember to forget.

CHAPTER SIX

Our Prison Song

You probably think the punishment I chose for Drover was too harsh. I mean, what could be more painful than spending the rest of his day alone with *himself*? I hate to be severe with the men, but if their leader doesn't set standards and enforce justice, who will do it? It's not my favorite part of this job, but it has to be done.

Anyway, I left the runt to his own boring company and went down to my office in the Security Division's Vast Office Complex, rode the elevator up to the twelfth floor, and spent the afternoon going over reports.

I was bent over my desk, studying spread-sheets...okay, maybe I was sprawled across my desk and dozing, but who wouldn't have dozed?

Deadly wasp poison will bring any dog to his nose.

It will bring a dog to his *knees*, let us say, and sleep is the best cure.

The point is that I had slipped into a few moments of healing sleep and was giving my body time to recover from the Wasp Attacks, when someone walked into my office.

"Knock, knock? Oh, there you are, and I guess you've been asleep."

I sat up. "What makes me think you were asleep? And who are you?"

"Well, I'm Drover. Remember me?"

I studied his face. "Oh yes, of course. We served together on a submarine, right?"

"What submarine?"

"Or was it a tug boat? What was your name again?"

"Drover. Drover with a D."

I struggle to my feet and took a few steps. "Oh yes, a sawed-off, stub-tailed little mutt?"

"Well, I'm not proud of my tail, but I guess that's who I am. Hey, you're talking better now."

"Thanks, and you're talking pretty well yourself. Good for you. Where are we?"

"Under the gas tanks."

I glanced around and noticed that everything seemed, well, familiar. "Oh, I see. Hmmm, yes.

I must have drifted into a light doze."

"Yeah, for about five hours. Hank, we need to talk."

"I agree. You know, the worst part of this job is that I rarely have time to talk to the men. Here, pull up a chair, sit down, make yourself comfortable." He sat down and so did I. "What shall we talk about?"

"Your wasp stings."

"My what?"

"You got stung and your mouth swole up, remember?"

"Oh yes, it's coming back now. I could hardly talk."

He hung his head and a look of sadness washed over his face. "Yeah, I laughed and made fun of you. I'm ashamed of myself!"

"Oh, don't worry about it. I'm feeling fine, and to be honest, it was one of the dumbest things I ever did. That's not your fault."

"Yeah, but there's more." He seemed to be fighting back tears.

"More?"

"Yeah, I told Pete."

A buzz of electricity shot down my spine. "You told the cat?"

He bobbed his head up and down and a tear

spilled out of his eye. "I did, and I even imitated the way you talked."

"You imitated...what do you mean?"

"Well, yo mouff wath all swowen up and you talked fummy, wike dis. And I talked that way for Pete."

"Yes, yes? And how did the little sneak respond?"

Drover shook his head. "I can't say it."

"Out with it, son, I must know."

"Well...he laughed his head off."

"Pete laughed at my misfortune?"

"Yeah, he loved it and now I feel awful. I'm so ashamed!"

I leaped to my feet and began pacing, as I often do when the Mouse Trap of Life has just snapped me on the nose. "Drover, this is worse than I could have imagined. You ratted to the cat!"

"I know!"

"You gave him Top Secret information, and even worse, you made him happy! You ought to be ashamed of yourself."

"I am, and I've already said it three times."

"Well, say it three more times."

He gave his head a hard shake. "No, that's not enough. I need to pay a heavier price."

"What do you mean?"

He didn't answer, but got up and made his way to the southeast angle-iron leg of the gas tank frame. There, he...this was really strange and I could hardly believe my eyes...he put his nose into the corner!

"I'll stay here until I get rid of the guilt, even if it takes two years. And you can watch the whole thing."

It took me a moment to recover from the shock. "Two years? Gee, that's a heavy load of guilt."

"Yeah, it's awful. What a louse I turned out to be!"

"No question about that, but...two years? I'm not sure we can spend that much time on your punishment."

"Okay, two weeks."

"Two weeks sounds better, but, still, we've got a busy schedule ahead of us."

"Two hours?"

"Drover, I'm a very busy dog and...let me tell you something." I paced over to his cell and spoke to him through the bars. "As a matter of fact, I also have a confession to make."

"You do?"

"Yes. See, I tricked you into snapping those wasps, expecting that you'd get stung."

"You did?"

"Absolutely. It was a dirty trick for a friend to play on a friend."

"Yeah, it really was. And you're ashamed of yourself too?"

"Drover, I've spent hours, feeling like a louse."

"Gosh, that's kind of weird, both of us feeling like louses."

"It is, and here's what we're going to do about it." I unlocked the cell next to Drover's, stepped into its dark cold interior, and put my nose into the northeast corner. "There. We will both submit ourselves to punishment for *two whole minutes*."

I heard him gasp in astonishment. "Oh my gosh, I never thought I'd see this!"

"Yes, well, we both deserve the punishment, son—me for trying to trick a friend, and you for giving pleasure to our worst enemy."

"I guess you're right. See you later."

And with that, we entered into a Punishment Phase. The first minute passed very slowly, I mean, it was pure torment, and I wasn't sure I could survive another minute. I decided to break the silence.

"Drover? I've been thinking. From a certain perspective, what we're doing here seems a little odd, don't you think?"

"Yeah, you might even call it weird."

"Exactly. That was the very word that came to my mind. So, as long as we're being weird, why don't we do a song about it?"

"A song about being weird?"

"Right. We'll make it up as we go along, and

here's the title: 'We Should Try Not To Be Any Weirder Than We Are Right Now.'"

"Gosh, you mean...just burst into song?"

"Right, exactly. They do it in books and movies all the time. If they can do it, we can do it. Just let your creative juices flow."

"I didn't know I had any."

"Drover, all dogs have them. We just don't use them very often."

"Well, okay...but it seems pretty weird."

"That's the whole point of the song. Prepare to burst into song!"

Right then and there, Drover and I burst into a song. Do we have time for you to listen to it? I guess we do. Roll the tape.

We Should Try Not to be Any Weirder Than We Are Right Now

Hank
We should try not to be any weirder than we
    are right now, today.
It'll take a little effort but I think we can do it
    all right, okay?

Drover
Yeah, a lot of dogs and people too
Wouldn't understand the things we do.

Hank
Two dogs locked in jail like this
Might strike someone as silliness.

Hank and Drover
We should try not to be
Any weirder than we are right now.
We should try not to be
Any weirder than we are right now.

Drover
There are some things that we can't discuss
With anyone but the two of us.

Hank
We're lucky that no one is here.
It could pull the plug on our career.

Hank and Drover
We should try not to be any weirder than we
    are right now, today.
It'll take a little effort but I think we can do it
    all right, okay?

Wow, was that an awesome song or what?
And don't forget that we made it up on the spot,
while serving Punishment Time in prison.
   But wait...what was that?
   All at once, the silence of the dungeon was

broken by a voice—not mine and not Drover's. It was the voice of some kind of Mysterious Visitor, some shadowy being who had somehow gained access to the prison and was...I had no idea what he might be doing, but I heard his voice and it caused the hair on my neck to stand straight up.

Here's what he said, a direct quote as though he had said it himself, word for word. This creepy voice said, "My goodness, I wonder what is going on around here?"

Wait, hold everything. Did you happen to notice the whiney tone of the mysterious voice? Maybe not, because you weren't there, but I sure noticed, and it reminded me a whole lot of a certain...

CHAPTER SEVEN

I Run Afoul of Radar Woman

Slowly, very slowly, I moved my head to the left, until my gaze fell upon A CAT. He wore an insolent smirk on his insolent smirking mouth and he was rubbing against the northwest angle-iron leg of the gas tank frame—and purring.

My eyes grew wide and burst into flame, and I heard a deadly growl gurgling in the deeps of my depths. "You!"

"Hello, Hankie, I hear that you, tee hee, had a bad experience playing with wasps."

"Oh yeah? Well, you're fixing to have a worse experience if you don't scram."

He fluttered his cattish eyes. "Now, now, Hankie. I was concerned and wanted to check on your condition."

"Lies, Pete. You were spying on us. Go ahead and admit it."

"Very well, Hankie, I was spying on you. Eavesdropping, actually."

"Next question: Did you eavesdrop on our song?"

"Why, yes, I did hear the song, and Hankie, I must tell you, it was amazing, one of the most moving performances I've ever heard."

This wasn't what I had expected, and it caught me a little off guard. "Are you being sincere or is this some kind of trickery?"

He rolled his gaze toward the sky. "Sincere, Hankie, straight from the heart. The harmony was so...so...so sweet!"

I glanced at Drover. He seemed puzzled too. "Well...thanks. We were kind of proud of it."

Drover nodded and grinned. "Yeah, and we didn't even practice."

Pete's mouth dropped open. "No rehearsals? Astonishing! Never in all my born days did I expect to hear such a masterpiece." In a grand gesture, he swept his paw through the air. "Two dogs, standing with their noses in the corner... *and singing about how weird they are*! Wa-hahahahahaha!"

He shrieked with irreverent laughter, and suddenly the world went red. I shot a glance at my assistant. "Did you hear that?"

"Oh yeah, he's making fun!"

"Exactly. We've been duped. Battle stations! Arm bombs and missiles, lock and load, stand by to launch all dogs!"

"Git 'im, Hankie, git 'im!"

Kitty had already scrammed and was racing toward the house. I hit the Launch Button and exploded out of my prison cell, oh you should have been there to see it! Smoke, flames, jet engines, the whole nine yards of sounds and smells that bring a rush of meaning into a dog's life.

With Drover's shouts of encouragement ringing in my ears, I went roaring out of our Vast Office Complex, past Emerald Pond, up the hill, and all the way to the house. I arrived just in time to see the little slacker scramble over the fence and take refuge in the yard—where, by the way, he paused long enough to *stick out his tongue at me*.

Perhaps he thought I wouldn't dare to enter Forbidden Territory and he would be safe. Ha. You know, cats have a primitive form of intelligence that allows them to scheme and stir up trouble, but they just don't understand dogs. Fellers, once we've warmed up the jets, it's not easy to turn 'em off.

I flew over the fence and had the great

satisfaction of seeing the look of surprise on Kitty's face. He was stunned and I loved it. I hit the ground running, turned on Vizrad, and locked the target into the computer. I had him in my sights and was about to...

Huh?

Someone appeared to be walking down the sidewalk, in a position directly between me and the cat. Unless I hit the Abort switch, we might have a collision. In combat, these things come at us like bullets flying past our ears, and we have to make instant decisions.

My instant decision was to plow through all obstacles and wreck the cat.

Oops. The obstacle turned out to be Slim Chance. He seemed to carrying a basket and was walking toward the house. Alas, I clipped him on the back of his knees and, well, he took a spill in the grass.

I stopped and took a closer look. Good grief, he was covered with...what was that stuff? It was yellow and slimy. I moved closer.

Sniff, sniff.

Okay, apparently he had gathered the eggs for Our Beloved Ranch Wife and was on his way to the house to deliver them, only he, uh, lost his footing and took a dive into the grass.

Well, you know me. When one of my guys

goes down, I'll be the first one on the scene to render aid and omelet...aid and comfort, that is. I'll be the first one there to aid in the cleanup.

Naturally, I felt terrible. After all, it had been partly my fault. I shut down the jets, cancelled the mission, and rushed to his side. He was a pitiful sight, with egg mess splattered on the front of his shirt and even dripping down his cheek. It touched my slurp...my heart, that is.

Poor Slim, my poor wounded omelet! My poor wounded *comrade*, let us say. I stepped forward and began giving him Emergency CPR licks to his face and shirt.

Why the shirt? Well, it was covered with egg mess, and bachelor cowboys need help with their personal appearance, right? You bet. Someone needs to keep them clean and tidy.

Also...well, no dog in his right mind would let such a delicious mess go to waste. Therefore, I licked and slurped and...

He shoved me away. "Quit!" At the same moment, I heard a voice behind me.

"Slim Chance, what have you done to my eggs! And what is that dog doing in my yard!"

Yipes!

I recognized the voice. It belonged to Radar Woman, She Who Sees Everything. I shot a

glance to the right and saw her standing on the porch with her hands parked on her hips, always an omelet sign. An *ominous* sign, let us say.

Actually, she had only one hand parked on her hip, because the other held her broom. That was a vital piece of information that somehow flew right past me. Had I noticed the Dreaded Broom,

I would have...

Actually, I would have done exactly what I did. I didn't care about the Dreaded Broom! I returned to the vital business of reviving my poor fallen omelet, as though there would be no tomorrow.

There almost *was* no tomorrow. I mean, she was really steamed about the busted eggs and me being in her yard, and maybe she'd seen me chasing her pampered little crook of a cat too. That would be typical because she sees EVERYTHING.

Anyway, I was doing CPR on Slim's shirt, and we're talking about totally absorbed in Selfless Service, when the broom came down across my back.

Whack!

"Hank, get out of my yard and stop being mean to the cat!"

Stop being mean to the...oh brother! What did I tell you? She sees everything, nobody's safe around her—only let me point out that she *didn't* see everything. She totally missed that her precious kitty had spied on me and Drover and had ridiculed one of our most touching musical creations.

The cat can do anything around here and get away with it, but all I have to do is...never mind.

She swatted me good and when I saw the

broom going up for a second shot, I abandoned Slim and raced toward a clump of vegetation near the northwest corner of the house. There, I hunkered down and peered through the iris plants to see if Sally May was in pursuit, when it dawned on me...

Iris patch? Slowly, I slid my gaze around to the right and saw...the cat. It was Pete, broadcasting his usual annoying smirk, only multiplied times five. He fluttered his eyelids and said, "My, she certainly delivers a blow with that broom, doesn't she?"

My lips leaped into a snarl. "How would you like to climb a tree?"

"Well, Hankie, I guess that depends on how many times you want to get flogged by the broom."

I cut my eyes from side to side. "Good point."

"Goodbye, Hankie, and by the way..." He whispered behind his paw, "It really was a nice little song. Thanks for sharing."

For a moment of heartbeats, as we stood nose to nose, I did a rapid calculation on the Ratio of Pain To Pleasure, in case I decided to give him the thrashing he so richly deserved. Data Control crunched the numbers and flashed a solution: "BETTER NOT."

So I delivered one last crushing message.

"You'll pay for this, you little snot!"

Just as the last word crossed my lips, Sally May's broom appeared above my head. I hit Afterburners on all engines and went roaring away. But here's the good part. Hee hee. I escaped but guess who got whacked by the broom. PETE! Either he didn't see it coming or was too lazy to move, and old Sally May really drilled him.

I heard the sweet music of his response: "Reeer, hisssss!"

It didn't heal all of my wounds, but it was a good start. Hee hee!

CHAPTER EIGHT

I Go Searching For Drover

Well, the unfortunate events in the yard did nothing to improve my reputation around headquarters. Sally May was mad again. Even Slim was mad, and his shirt was a mess. I mean, before the accident, it had been the color of faded blue-denim. Now, it had changed into a kind of sickening shade of yellow.

Who got all the blame? ME, of course, even though Slim hadn't been paying attention to…okay, it was mostly my fault, might as well admit it.

You're probably asking yourself, "Where was Drover while all this was going on?" Great question. If you recall, when the fiasco began, he was the one who was egging me on by saying, "Git 'im, Hankie, git 'im!" He does that quite often, and there seems to be something about those particular words that...well, they strike matches in the mind of a dog. But the odd part is that, once Drover starts a fire, he tends to vanish without a trace.

So there's the answer. He vanished without a trace.

By the way, you might have noticed that I injected a little humor into my otherwise gloomy report. See, I said that Drover was "egging me on." Did you get it? Egging me on, broken eggs? Ha ha. See, Slim fell in the grass and...maybe you got it.

The point is that Drover had gone M.I.A., and in case you're not familiar with technical terms, M.I.A. means...I've forgotten what it means. Huh. I had it right on the tick of my tock. It's really annoying when this happens.

Never mind.

We'll switch to another technical term, A.W.O.L. That is our shorthand term for "A Weasel Often Lollygags," and it captures the deeper layers of so-forth in these situations, when Drover behaves like a little weasel and lollygags his way out of danger. That's A.W.O.L.

I hope you don't get lost in these technical terms. To be honest, I get a kick out of using them.

Anyway, I went looking for Drover, is the point, and had a pretty good idea where to find him, in his Secret Sanctuary, the machine shed. I rumbled up to the crack between the big sliding doors and poked my head inside. "Drover? I know you're in there."

I was surprised when a voice said, "No, I'm not here. Check the gas tanks."

Hmm. That was odd. I'd been sure I would find him in the machine shed, but maybe not. I hiked down to our office under the gas tanks and got another surprise: two empty gunny sack beds and no sign of Drover. He was gone. A cold chill scampered down my backbone. Maybe the little mutt had wandered off or maybe he'd been kidnapped by…

Wait, hold everything. Had you forgotten the voice in the machine shed? Let's pull up that file and listen to it again.

"No, I'm not here. Check the gas tanks."

Don't you get it? Someone had spoken those words, someone who was hiding inside the machine shed, and you'll never guess who or whom that might have been. Hang on, this is pretty shocking.

It must have been Drover!

I stormed back to the machine shed, and this

time, I stepped inside. "Drover? Report to the front immediately, and that is a direct order."

Again, I heard a voice. "No, I'm not here."

"Drover, I checked the gas tanks and you weren't there either."

"How about the calf shed?"

Hm, I hadn't thought of that. Drover had been known to hide in the calf shed. "Okay, I'll be right back."

I slipped back outside and began trotting down to...I did a one-eighty turn and marched back into the machine shed. "Drover, enough of this nonsense! Report to the front at once, or you will be fed to the buzzards!"

I heard a small voice. "Oh rats."

Moments later, he appeared out of the gloomy darkness of his sanctuary. As he came padding up, I pulled myself up to my full height and pointed to a spot on the cement floor. "Sit." He sat and hung his head. "Did you actually think I was dumb enough to fall for that trick?"

"No. I was shocked that it worked."

"It worked because I trusted you. I had faith that my assistant would never pull such a cheap trick on me."

"Well, you pull cheap tricks on me all the time."

"Drover, this is a ridiculous conversation. Let's

forget about our history of cheap tricks and start
all over from scratch." All at once, he hiked up his
hind leg and began scratching his ear. "Why are
you doing that in the middle of my lecture?"

"I don't know. You said 'scratch' and I felt a

powerful urge to scratch."

"All right, let me rephrase it. Let's start all over from *un-scratch*."

He stopped scratching and blinked his eyes. "You know, I think that worked."

"Good. No more shabby tricks, no more guilt, no more scratching during business hours. It's a brand new day."

He glanced around. "Yeah, but it's almost evening."

"Exactly my point, and I'm glad you mentioned it. We have to set up a Coon Patrol at the cake house tonight and we're looking for a volunteer for the first shift." His gaze wandered. "It could lead to a nice promotion."

"Oh goodie."

I gave him a pat on the shoulder. "I like your attitude, soldier."

He stood up and began limping. "But you know...ouch, boy, this old leg has been giving me fits." He went two steps and dropped like a chunk of cement. "Oh, drat the luck, there it went! Oh, my leg!"

"Drover, watch out for that black widow spider!"

Heh. He sprang to his feet and headed for the door, but slowed to a walk, then stopped. "You know, the leg's feeling a little better now, but I'm scared of coons."

"Not a problem, son. If a coon shows up, come fetch me. We'll give him a thrashing and send him on his way."

He gave me a sulking glare. "There wasn't a spider. You tricked me again."

"Drover, I tricked you for your own good. This time tomorrow, you'll be glad it worked out this way."

"I doubt that."

"What?"

"I said...oh goodie."

"That's the spirit."

Pretty touching scene, huh? You bet. Any time I can provide encouragement to the men, I'm glad to do it. Teamwork. It's one of the things that make this old life worth living.

Well, the sun went down at its usual time for that time of year, around seven o'clock, and darkness began spreading across the ranch. At 0730, I escorted Drover up the hill north of the corrals and hand-delivered him to a spot right in front of the cake house door.

"All right, trooper, you will establish a Security Zone right here. Don't leave your post and don't fall asleep."

"Oh darn."

"I beg your pardon?"

"I said, you bet, no problem."

"If anyone tries to enter the building, come wake me up."

"You'll be asleep?"

"Absolutely not. I'll be up most of the night, catching up on paperwork."

"You said to wake you up."

I gave him a steely glare. "I was misquoted. Beware of anything you hear, Drover. Our enemies are very clever and they never rest."

I left him there, whimpering and complaining, and returned to the office to face the mountain of reports stacked up on my...*someone was sitting in my office!* I stopped in my tracks and studied the shadowy form.

Had I forgotten an appointment with someone? Or was this some kind of intruder who had slipped into the building undetected?

At that point, I didn't know. And neither do you.

CHAPTER NINE

Eddy Walks Into My Trap

Are you still with me? Good, because I might need some help with this one.

Okay, it appeared that I had just stumbled into a break-in by the Charlie Monsters, and some kind of carbon-based life form was sitting in my office. In the half-darkness, I could see only one of them, but that didn't mean there weren't two or five or twenty.

Don't forget, the Charlies are masters of disguise, and over my long career, I had seen many examples of their tradecraft: dressing up in chicken suits, masquerading as postal employees and wild turkeys, you name it. We'd even heard reports that they sometimes sprayed themselves with invisible ink.

That's the frightening thing about the Charlies. If you see one, there might be ten others that are blending into the surroundings. That's scary.

It appeared that they had staked out the building, see, and once everyone had left, they swooped in, hot-wired the elevator, and broke down the office door.

Who knows what they were after this time— top secret files, reports, spreadsheets, maps that showed the location of every buried bone on the ranch, our geopolitical strategy for dealing with cats. The possibilities were chilling.

A lot of your ordinary mutts would have sold out right there and left the building. Not me. Hey, I don't look for opportunities to go up against the Charlies, but when the needle of Life's Compass points to me, I go in with guns blazing.

That's what I did, laid down a withering barrage of Alert and Alarm Barks. "Freeze, turkey, on the ground, hands up, move it!" I charged into the office. The guy was so shocked, he hit the ground and covered his eyes with his paws, and screeched, "Help, murder, mayday!"

I crept forward and noticed...hmm, in certain ways, the culprit resembled...well, Drover, but I had just left him at the cake house. Good grief, were they dressing up in Drover suits? What would they think of next?

"Okay, pal, who are you, how did you get into this office, and what are you doing here?"

He didn't say a word but slithered the top-half of his body underneath Drover's gunny sack bed. I could see it quivering, and at that point, I began to wonder...

Huh?

Okay, relax. Ha ha. Let's take a moment to decompose. *Decompress*, I guess it should be, decompress. This will come as a big surprise. See, it actually *was* Drover, not an enemy spy wearing a Drover suit. Ha ha.

Whoo! All the air hissed out of my chest of drawers and I almost collapsed as all the muscles in my body went into the Stand-Down response. "Drover, what are you doing here? I left you to guard the cake house and you beat me back to the office!"

One eye peeked out from under the gunny sack. "Well, I heard a sound."

"You heard a sound. Okay, let's get this over with. What exactly did you hear?"

"Well, just as you were leaving, I heard these...these footsteps in the dark, and I figured you'd want to know."

I took a deep breath of carbon diego and tried to calm the pounding of my heart. "Did you catch sight of anyone who might have been the source of those alleged footsteps?"

"Well...not exactly."

"Did you see anyone at all?"

"Let me think here. Yeah, I saw you, but you were leaving."

I stepped forward, took a bite on his gunny sack, and jerked it off the quivering jelly of his whatever. "Did it ever occur to you that you were hearing *my footsteps*?"

He blinked his eyes several times. "I'll be derned, I never thought of that."

"Meathead! Get yourself back to the cake house and...never mind, I'll take the first shift. And Drover, this WILL go into my report, and you WILL be written up with ten Chicken Marks."

"Oh no, not that!"

"Yes, and you're just lucky to be getting off with only ten. Next time, it'll be ten thousand."

What can you say? Not much. Maybe the runt was doing his best with limited gifts, but his best just didn't cut it in the world I occupied. Where I live and work every day...never mind. Fuming about Drover is a waste of time.

I left him on his gunny sack and hiked up the hill to the cake house. There, I established a Secured Zone around the door: five paces north of the door, five paces south. Nothing and no one would go in or out of that space.

I had marched my route several times when I began to realize...this was really boring.

I couldn't imagine keeping up this routine all night long, but I didn't dare allow myself to fog asnerk...to fall asleep, that is. Somewho I herd to stay awerp...had to stay awake and fight against battle fatigue and snorking pork chops in the whooping crane pretzels....zzzzzzz.

Okay, let's be honest. Just for a few minutes, I slipped into a phase of dozing. I'm sure it was caused by my near-fatal encounter with the yellow jacket wasps. No, really, I'm serious. That yellow jacket venom is extremely powerful, and it's a wonder I had survived.

But the point here, the impointant poink, is that I slipped into a light dozing situation and was awakened by a series of odd thudding sounds: "Pah-DOO-pah. Pah-DOO-pah." I rushed to the screen of my mind and called up Diagnostics. Data Control came back with a flashing message:

**"A series of odd thudding
sounds, unidentified."**

I pushed myself up to a standing position, cracked open both eyes, and did a Visual Sweep of the entire area. What I saw in the half-darkness was a little guy, sitting on his haunches and throwing a red rubber ball against the side of the barn.

Are you following this? Okay, let me explain. The rubber ball was making those "odd thudding sounds," don't you see. The "pah" came when the ball hit the ground, the "doo" came when the ball bounced off the side of the barn, and the final "pah" came when it hit the ground again. At that point, the intruder caught the ball in his hands and went through the entire process again.

No dog, cat, horse, or cow could toss a ball in that manner, and that gave me my first clue in this case: the suspect was not a dog, cat, horse, or cow. The second clue followed immediately: the guy was wearing a black bandit's mask over his eyes.

Do you get it now? I had set up a Secured Zone to intercept thieving raccoons, and here was one right in front of me! He had walked right into my trap and was throwing a ball against the side of the cake house.

I went straight into Warning Growls and Hair Liftup. He caught the ball and swiveled his head around. "Oh, hi. How's it going? Long night, huh?" He tossed the ball at the barn. Pah-doo-pah.

There was something familiar about his voice. I squinted my eyes and took a closer look. "Eddy?"

I rose to my full height of massiveness, lumbered over to him, and studied his facial so-forths. Sure enough, I knew the guy.

Remember Eddy the Rac? He was a little shrimp of an orphan coon that Slim and I rescued from a pack of stray dogs. Slim kept him around as a pet, until he became such a home-wrecker and pain in the neck, we turned him loose and sent him back to the wild. Now and then he showed up around headquarters, and we could always be sure of one thing: any time Eddy showed up, trouble wasn't far behind.

And here he was, back again. "Eddy, what do you think you're doing? You're in a Secured Area."

"It's a barn."

"It's a barn that happens to be under tight security."

"Playing ball."

"I see that you're playing ball and that's nice. Coons need to stay busy with something."

He threw the ball up in the air and caught it. "Right. Moonlight Madness. Can't sit still, got to boogey."

I paced around him and gave him a steady gaze. He didn't seem as concerned about this deal as he should have been. After throwing the ball in the air several times, now he was rolling it around in his hands. I had to admit, he had an amazing pair of hands.

"Eddy, I've got nothing personal against you. It just happens that we're on opposite sides of the law. Coons are not allowed anywhere close to this barn. For security reasons, I can't tell you why, so you'll just have to take my word for it."

"Fresh cow feed?"

I flinched. "That is supposed to be classified

information."

"Smell."

I lifted my nose and drew in air samples. Hmm. They carried the strong, nutty smell of... well, ten tons of fresh cottonseed cake. "Okay, smart guy, you've got a good smeller. It makes me twice as suspicious about why you happen to be in front of this feed barn."

"Playing wall ball. Want to see?"

"No. I've already seen it."

"Great wall."

"It's a great wall, but there are plenty of other walls you could be using: the machine shed, the chicken house, the tool shed. I'd advise you to run along and..."

"Want to see a trick?"

"No. The point I'm making...what trick?"

He held up the ball in the fingers of his right hand. "Magic. Make the ball disappear, poof."

I had to laugh. "Eddy, Eddy. You never grow up. Look, pal, I've studied your tactics and these so-called magic tricks are just part of your tired, sad routine. Nobody on this ranch believes in magic."

"Watch this." He held the ball in the fingers of his right hand, passed his left hand over the ball, then flung both hands into the air. The ball had...well, vanished, so to speak. "Hee hee.

Bingo. What do you think?"

"It's a variation of the old coin trick, Eddy. I've seen you do it before. It's not magic, it's trickery."

"Where's the ball?"

"Probably behind your ear."

He brushed his paws across his ears. "Nope."

"Just as I thought. It's concealed in one of your arm pits."

He raised both arms. "Nope. Hee hee."

"Just as I suspected. That leaves only one place, pal. You're sitting on it." He stared off into space and didn't respond, so I knew I'd nailed him. "Stand up, Eddy."

"Huh?"

"Stand up."

"Now?"

"That's the order, stand up now."

"Darn."

Heh heh. I had exposed the little fraud.

CHAPTER TEN

The Chase-Ball Olympics

I magine Eddy thinking that he could fool me with the Disappearing Ball trick! Ha. Sneaky little raccoons who think they can fool the Head of Ranch Security eventually learn a hard lesson: It can't be done. No coon can out-fox a dog, not when I'm the dog.

See, Eddy had overplayed his hand, and that's one of the tendencies I had spotted in our Profiles of Coon Behavior. They can do amazing things with those little hands, and they have the kind of mind that's good at producing schemes and tricks, but the combination of the two makes them overconfident.

They get to thinking they're smarter than they actually are, don't you see, and that's always a mistake, thinking you're the smartest guy in the room.

Although, come to think about it, in my case, it's usually true.

But back to the interrogation. I had pushed Little Houdini to the point where he was out of hiding places for the so-called vanishing ball, and I ordered him to stand up.

Disappointment showed all over his face, but I remained firm. "Stand up, Eddy."

"You're tough."

"Of course I'm tough. It's part of my job."

"Hard to fool you."

"Exactly right. Now, are you going to stand up or do you need help?"

He sighed and pushed himself up to a standing position. My gaze went straight to the spot where…I couldn't believe it. There was no ball!

I lumbered over to him. "Okay, Shorty, that's enough. Where's the ball?"

He made a little basket with his hands and looked into it. "In there? What do you think?"

"Hurry up."

He pulled his hands apart and threw them into the air. "Nope. Wait." He reached out his hand and touched the back of my left ear, withdrew the hand and held up…a red rubber ball! "Hee hee. Behind your ear all along."

"Hey Eddy, I don't know how you did that, but the ball wasn't behind my ear."

"Magic. You ever chase a ball?"

"What?"

"Chase a ball. What do you think?"

I paced a few steps away and looked up at the stars. There were many of them, all up in the sky. "Eddy, I don't know how to say this in a nice way, so I'll just blurt it out. I'm an important dog. I run this entire ranch. I have a real job. Do you have any idea what that means?"

"Guard dog, bark, stuff like that?"

"That's a tiny part of it. I work eighteen hours a day, which is something you've never done in your entire life, and something you will never understand. The point is that, no, I don't chase balls. It's a silly, insignificant amusement for mutts that have nothing better to do."

"Fun. Watch." He rolled the ball across the ground, about five feet, then scampered after it, picked it up in his mouth, and brought it back. He dropped it at my feet. "Cool or what?"

I shook my head. "Eddy, you have too much time on your hands. You think that's a big deal, chasing a ball?"

"Try it."

"I will not try it." He reached out a foot and gave the ball a gentle kick. It rolled about ten inches. "So this is...what? Some kind of challenge? Okay, pal, just for the record..." I walked over to the ball, picked it up in my mouth, and dropped it at his feet. "I fetched the ball. It was no big deal. That's the end of it."

"You're good." Eddy gave the ball another kick, this one harder, and the ball went fifteen or twenty feet.

I glared into his face. "Eddy, I'm done. I'm not going to...okay, one more time, but this is *it*." I trotted after the ball and brought it back. "Now, if you'll excuse me..."

Eddy picked up the ball, drew back his arm, and threw it out into the darkness. Then he gave me a cunning little grin. "Race you to it!" He darted after the ball.

Let's get something straight. I shouldn't have cared about this silliness. In fact, I *didn't* care about it, but...well, he had more or less thrown down the goblet and challenged me to a test of skill. And all at once, it seemed important that I respond.

He had gotten a head start, but deep in my heart, I felt I could beat him. I had pretty amazing speed in a short sprint, don't forget, and that's one talent coons don't have. In the fall,

they're lard-fat and their short legs aren't suited for sprinting. Me? I *am* suited for sprinting, big time, any time.

I hit Turbos and raced after the ball, caught up with Eddy, blew right past him, and found the ball without the slightest difficulty. Eddy arrived, huffing and puffing. "Awesome. Thought I could beat you. No more, I quit."

There was a moment of silence. "Actually, that was more fun than I expected. Maybe you could throw it one more time."

He stared at me. "Nah. I'm tired, bushed."

"Look, it doesn't have to be a contest. I don't want to sound cruel, Eddy, but you throw a whole lot better than you run. I'll give you a few lessons on how to fetch a ball."

"Neat. Okay."

He picked up the ball, held it in his busy fingers for a moment, then drew back and threw it quite a bit farther than his first throw. I went after it like a dog after a rabbit and snagged it on the second bounce.

I met Eddy about halfway and dropped the ball at his feet. He was impressed. "Wow. Again?"

"No, I have things to do. Oh, what the heck, let's try it one more time, but this time, give it a ride."

"Throw hard?"

"Right. I want a real test of my limits."

"Cool." He stood on his back legs and began limbering up his throwing arm, either his right or left arm, I don't recall which. He spun his arm in a circle and gave me a wink. "Deep center field. Downtown."

I got down in my Starting Crouch. "Let 'er rip, son."

He let 'er rip, all right, and I let ME rip, exploding out of the starting blocks like a rocket. Smoke, flames, the whole deal. Streaking through the darkness, I went to Ear Lift-up and waited to hear the "thud" of the ball hitting the ground.

That was part of my stragedy, see. When a dog is running wide open, he can't look up and watch the ball, but it really doesn't matter. If he knows the general direction of the path of the vectors of the trajectory of the so-forth (I did), then he runs at top speed and waits to hear the thud of the ball when it hits the ground. At that point, he switches on Earatory Scanners and follows instruments to the bouncing target.

When it's done right, and when the dog is in top fiscal condition, he can cover an enormous distance and pounce upon the prize before it stops rolling.

Is that impressive or what? You bet, and don't forget, this was happening in the dark. Well, not total darkness (we had a half-moon), but pretty dark.

Where were we? Oh yes, the ball. I went streaking southeast, toward the center of headquarters, and kept waiting to hear the sound of the ball hitting the ground, at which point I would home in on the "thud," do a course correction, and move into the Phase Two procedure.

I ran and waited, waited and ran.

Well, I had told Eddy to give the ball a ride and he'd sure done that. The little guy had quite an arm, and the next thing I knew...holy smokes, I had run all the way back to headquarters and was standing not far from the chicken house. And the ball still hadn't hit the ground! Amazing.

I was in the process of searching the heavens for something round and red, when I was startled by the sound of a voice close by. It said, and this is a direct quote, it said, "What's all the darned noise out here?"

You probably think I jumped out of my skin in surprise. No, and here's why. Number One, there was something familiar about the voice: the speaker whistled when he pronounced an "S." Number Two, this was all happening in close proximity to the chicken house. And Number Three...

There wasn't a Number Three, but two were enough for our Voice Recognition Algorithm. Here, let's look at these two equations:

Voice + Chicken House = Chicken Voice.

Chicken Voice + Whistles = J.T. Cluck.

Do you get it now? Is that amazing or what? You bet, and don't forget that this all occurred in total darkness—no moon whatsoever, I mean, not even a sliver. Black dark.

Anyway, it was my bad luck to have run into J.T. Cluck, the Head Rooster, on a dark night when I had important work to do. I could see him in the light of the half-moon. And here he came. "What's a-going on around here?" He stopped a few feet from me, cocked his head to the side, and gave me the Rooster Eye. "Oh, it's you."

"J.T., I don't have time to talk."

"Good. Neither do I. What's a-going on around here?"

"I'm looking for a red rubber ball."

He stared at me. "Well, that's dumb. Why would you be looking for a ball in the middle of the night?"

"Sorry, I can't reveal that information. It's classified and none of your business."

"Well, whoop-tee-do. Did you happen to notice that it's dark out here? Some of us try to sleep when the sun goes down, but it ain't easy when there's a dog outside, banging around and making..."

Suddenly, his voice just quit, shut off, and I noticed that his head had dropped down on his chest and his eyes slammed shut. It appeared that he had fallen asleep in mid-sentence, and we're talking about conked out.

Okay, this is a common characteristic of chickens. When darkness falls, they also fall—asleep. And it doesn't seem to matter where they are.

Good. This gave me a perfect opportunity to slip away and avoid a long, boring conversation with one of the most boring personalities I'd ever known. J.T. wasn't a bad guy, but after you'd heard all his heartburn stories fifteen times, you found yourself wishing to avoid his company.

I edged away and began tip-toeing...

"Hey! Where do you think you're a-going?"

"You fell asleep in the middle of our conversation, and I have things to do."

"Hold your horses, pooch, I've got some information that you might find pretty interesting."

I walked back to him and studied his face. He seemed awake. "Okay, I'll give you three minutes. Talk."

"You said you was looking for a red rubber ball?"

"That's correct. Do you know anything about it?"

"Well, I might, sure might, but I never thought about it until just now."

"Can you hurry up?"

"Don't crowd me, pooch, you'll want to hear this." He hiked up his left leg and tucked it under his wing, which meant that he was standing on one leg. "It happened this very afternoon, pooch. Elsa come a-running up to me and she was all stirred up, clucking up a storm."

"Yes? She was stirred up. Go on."

"She was sure stirred up, and she come a-running up to me and she called out, 'Oh my, oh me, oh J.T.!' That's always the sign that she's seen something unusual."

"What was it?" He didn't answer and I saw why. He'd fallen asleep again and was even making some ridiculous little chicken snores. "Hey! Wake up and finish your story."

His eyes popped open and he flinched. "Worst heartburn since I ate that dad-ratted scorpion." He blinked his red rooster eyes and glanced around. "Who are you?"

"Never mind. Finish your story about Elsa. She was all stirred up."

"Oh yeah, and here's the good part." He leaned forward and dropped his voice. "She told me she'd found something that was *round* and *red*, and I've got a feeling it's the very thing you're a-looking for!"

CHAPTER ELEVEN

I Am Forced By Circumstances to Say "Please"

J.T.'s story didn't exactly add up, but I was curious to see where it would lead. After you've been in Security Work for a while, you learn that we often get our best leads...we've already covered that, so skip it.

I paced back and forth in front of the rooster. "Okay, J.T., we might be onto something here, but I need facts and details. Elsa found something round and red. What was it?"

"I wondered about that too, so I checked on it myself. Sometimes she gets her facts a little confused, if you know what I mean."

"What did she find?"

He gazed up to the sky. "Well...it was a tomater."

I stared at him, dumbfounded. "*A tomato*! I'm

98

not looking for a tomato, I'm looking for a red rubber ball!"

"Well, you don't need to screech. What I'm a-saying is that you might be looking for the wrong thing. Had you ever thought of that? They look pretty close to the same."

The air hissed out of my lungs. "Why do I bother talking to you? Go back to bed, get out of my sight before I do something crazy. Scram!"

He slunk back toward the chicken house, and I heard him mutter, "Boy, it sure don't pay to be friendly around here. I was just trying to help, never dreamed he'd bite my darned head off."

Oh brother. Well, I had wasted precious minutes trying to squeeze information out of a feather-brained rooster, but during my interrogation of the nitwit, my Earatory Scanners had continued operating...and they had picked up NO sound of the ball coming back to earth. What was going on around here? I mean, Eddy had a good throwing arm, but this was beginning to sound a little crazy. Balls that go up must come down.

You're probably wondering...why did I care? It was just an ordinary ball. It meant nothing to me, and yet...well, somehow it did. I wanted to find that ball and bring closure to the whole situation, and...I don't know, prove to a slippery little raccoon that I could handle anything he threw at me.

Maybe there was a little pride involved. Of course there was pride involved! Hey, I wasn't just thinking of myself. I was representing the entire Security Division, and you could take it even farther and say that I was representing dogs all over the world.

It was a HUGE responsibility, and I had to find that ball.

Okay, back to the hunt. Clearly, the ball couldn't possibly be in flight after so much time had eloped. In other words, it had returned to earth and was lying somewhere on the ground.

I called up Maps and Charts and tried to reconstroodle the flight path of the ball, using a mathematical process called "Strangulation." Wait. *"Triangulation,"* there we go. See, you construct a three-sided triangle in your mind and multiply the triangle times Apple Pi, which produces Apple Stroodle. Hencely, we have "reconstroodled" the strangularity of the...this is getting too complicated. Let's move on.

The point is that I was able to reconstroodle the flight path of Eddy's ball, and the calculations indicated that Splashdown occurred somewhere between my present location and the ranch

house...although it wouldn't have made a splash. Why? No water.

It doesn't matter. The ball had come down somewhere in this general area, and I would need some help to find it. I headed for the gas tanks in a brisk trot, rode the elevator up to the Twelfth Floor, and found my assistant just where I had expected to find him: sprawled like spilled milk across his gunny sack bed, twitching, squeaking, and grunting in his sleep.

"Drover, we've had an incident and I need some help."

He came roaring out of a dead sleep and squeaked, "Help, murder, mayday!" He leaped to his feet, turned three circles on his bed, crashed into the southeast angle-iron leg of the gas tanks, and collapsed on the ground.

"Drover, I really need...forget it."

Worthless. What else can you say? I needed his help, but getting "help" out of Drover is like...I don't know, trying to squeeze pineapple juice out of a rock, I suppose.

Remember that song we had performed only hours before, "We Should Try Not To Be Any Weirder Than We Are Right Now"? Well, that had become the Song of Drover's Life. He should have been singing it ten times every day. He should have posted the words on the bedroom wall, because there seemed to be no limit to his weirdness.

Oh well, I would have to rely on my own resources. I left the office and plunged into the enormous task of sniffing out the entire headquarters compound. I had retained a strong memory of the ball's scent and knew I would recognize it if I got within ten feet of it, but our headquarters compound covered a lot of area.

We're talking BIG, four or five acres that included the corrals, the chicken house, Emerald Pond, the machine shed...big.

I laid out a grid in my mind and began working the grid in straight north-south lines, back and forth, trotting, sniffing, nose to the ground, and after fifteen minutes...it seemed hopeless.

Wait! All at once I was sneezed by an idea that might very well blow the case wide open. Here, check this out.

- Who was the biggest snoop on our ranch?
- Who stayed awake all night, spying and eavesdropping?
- Who might have heard or seen the ball when it landed?
- Who might possess the crucial information on where it rolled to a stop?

Did you get the right answer? Here's a clue:

iris patch. Yes, Pete the Sneak. Mister Kitty Moocher. Sally May's rotten little cat.

If the ball landed anywhere within a mile of the iris patch, Kitty would know. Brilliant idea. The only trouble was...gag...I would have to do business with the little creep, and the very thought made me ill. Was I dog enough to humble myself and ask a cat for help?

This plunged me into a period of deep soul-searching of my soul. I paced and searched and probed the depths of my Inner Bean, and after several minutes, the answer came, loud and clear.

NO, OF COURSE NOT, NEVER EVER, NIX DICE, NO DEAL!!

But I would have to do it anyway.

Sigh.

I lifted my head to a proud angle, pointed myself toward the east, and marched up the house to the hill...up the hill to the house, let us say. At the yard gate, I stopped. The house was dark, all its inhabitants enjoying a peaceful sleep. For them, Life was simple. How nice. My life was full of heavy moral decisions and compromises.

I took a deep breath and worked up my courage. "Pete?" No answer. Typical. He would make me squirm. "Pete? I know you're there and

I know you're awake."

At last his voice came from the darkness, and I must admit, the whiney tone caused my lips to twitch. "My, my, it's Hankie the Wonderdog!"

"Pete, I know it's late, but could we have a word?"

"Oh, by all means. Which word shall we have? Let me think...oh, here's one. It begins with a P and ends with an E."

"Panhandle?"

"Hankie, I don't think this is going to work."

"Okay, I know the word you have in mind, but...well, it's really hard for me to say."

"I know. Poor doggie."

"Here's an idea. Let's come back to it later. What do you think?"

"No."

"I can't say that word, Pete, just can't do it."

"Bye."

"Fine, you little creep!" I whirled around and marched...back to the gate. "Okay, you win, but I'd advise you not to gloat about it."

"What was the word, Hankie?"

I braced myself and spit it out. "Please."

"Again, louder."

"Please!"

"A little louder, Hankie."

I was only seconds away from an explosion

but caught myself just in time. "Pete, could we *please* have a word?" Boy, that really hurt.

"Well, I suppose we could."

Naturally, he took his sweet time. He slithered out of the iris patch and came rubbing his way down the fence, purring and holding his tail straight up in the air.

Have you ever wondered how cats learn how to walk that way? I've wondered about it, plenty. They must go to a special school or take private lessons to learn how to walk in a manner that makes everyone hate them on sight.

See, you don't have to meet a cat to know you're not going to like him. You just watch him walk.

You talk about self-control! It took everything I had to sit there and watch and wait for the little reptile to go through all his theatricals, but finally he arrived at the gate. There, he fluttered himself down into a sitting position, wrapped his tail around his back side, and gave me his patented insolent smirk (which drives me nuts, by the way).

"Well, Hankie, here I am and here you are. How strange that we should be meeting at this hour of the night. What's on your mind?"

And so it began, my appeal to the local cat for help in solving a case. I never thought I'd stoop so low and couldn't have predicted where it would lead.

Keep reading. I mean, you will never guess what came next.

CHAPTER TWELVE

Incredible Ending, Amazing

I glared at Kitty through the wire mesh in the gate. "What's on my mind? To be honest, I'm sitting here thinking about how much I hate waiting on a cat to show up for a meeting."

"I'm sure it must be annoying."

"It's worse than that. It eats my liver. And I haven't forgotten that little incident in the yard either."

He sputtered a laugh. "She really whopped you with that broom! But you know, Hankie, there's a simple solution: don't come into her yard."

"Never mind. I'm working on a case and I've hit a dead end. Unfortunately, you may be the only one on the ranch who can help." I began pacing back and forth in front of the cat and told him the whole story about Eddy and the ball. "He threw it high and long, and I know it must have come down somewhere around headquarters, but I can't find it."

He gave that some thought. "So...you were on guard duty but playing ball with a raccoon? Hankie, that doesn't sound like something you would do."

"I realize that, and it's not something I care to discuss. Get to the point. Did you see or hear the ball when it landed?"

"No. But I can tell you where it is."

I stopped pacing. "You can?"

He nodded and whispered behind his paw. *"Eddy didn't throw it.* He faked you out of your drawers and sent you on a wild goose chase."

"That's ridiculous! How dumb do you think I am?"

There was a long moment of silence. "Well, that's an interesting question and we can discuss it sometime, but I think you'll find Eddy inside the barn, probably eating feed cubes. The ball will be nearby."

Huh?

I had to sit down and think through this latest development. "Of course! Don't you get it? He's an untrustworthy little sneak and it was a rigged deal from the start. He lured me into playing his stupid little game, but, Pete, I *knew* there was something fishy about it. No kidding."

"Hmm. Knowing doesn't always help, I guess. Well! Maybe you'd better go check on the coon."

I moved closer to the fence and gave Kitty a hard glare. "Hey Pete, don't tell me my job. I'm on it, okay? Now, if you'll excuse me, I have to get back to work, before Eddy tears the feed barn to smithereens."

I had already hit Full Turbos and was roaring away from the scene when I heard the cat say, "Good luck, Hankie, and you're welcome."

Okay, maybe I could have gone back and thanked him, I mean, he had played a small but tiny part in breaking the case wide open. But I had Eddy on my mind and...well, who wants to thank a cat anyway? Not me.

I went streaking past the machine shed, past the chicken house, past the corrals, through a grove of chinaberry trees, and up the hill to the cake house. There, I throttled back to a walk and began thinking about what I might find.

Gulp.

We'd been through this before, you know, Eddy running wild in a feed barn. Nobody on our ranch had any problem with the idea of providing him or any other coon with snacks, or even feeding him through the winter. But Eddy couldn't be content with mere eating. Oh no, he would rip open one sack with his little dagger claws, eat a few pellets of feed, then move on down the line, ripping open one sack after another.

At the end of a busy night, he might leave a hundred pounds of loose feed scattered across the floor. He was a natural-born wrecker, is what he was, as well as a natural-born sneak, and...

Oh brother, I had posted myself on guard duty to *prevent* exactly that kind of disaster from happening, but somehow he had...

I prepared myself for the worst. It didn't take Eddy long to slash up a bunch of feed sacks, and if that happened, I was cooked, and I mean COOKED. Slim would...I didn't even want to imagine what Slim would do.

I'm saying all this to prepare you for a disaster that could end my career. It was *that* serious. I don't want to ruin your day, but we don't want to walk into this deal unprepared.

Okay, I crept toward the cake house and tried not to think about all the damage I would find, when all at once, I heard...voices? Yes, at least two voices. I stopped in my tracks and studied the situation, and was astounded by what I saw.

Eddy was sitting in front of the cake house, pitching THE RED RUBBER BALL in his hands, and talking to...you will not believe this...he was talking to Drover C. Dog!

Do you see the meaning of this? Actually, there were two meanings. First, Eddy was holding the ball, which meant that *he never threw it in the first place.* Didn't I tell you it was just a slimy trick? I'd suspected it from the very beginning.

And second...this one stretched my powers of belief...Drover had somehow managed to show up at the Guard Station, which he had abandoned hours ago!

How and why that happened, we will never know. Maybe he walked in his sleep. Maybe he got bored. Maybe he had lost what little mind he had left, but there he was, talking to one of the most notorious villains on the entire ranch.

I moved closer and listened.

Eddy: "Wow. You're good, know how to fetch, awesome. Try it again?"

Drover: "No, Hank might show up and...okay, let's try it one more time, but this time, really give it a ride."

"Throw hard?"

"Oh yeah, throw it to the moon. I bet I can find it."

"Cool. Here goes...to the moon!"

Are you shocked? I was. My assistant was playing fetch with the coon, and here's the rest of it. Eddy stood on his back legs and began limbering up his throwing arm, spun his arm in a circle, and gave it a mighty heave.

Drover yelled, "Here I go!" and went hopping down the hill. As a matter of fact, he was coming straight toward me. I rose to my feet and placed my enormous body in his path. "Halt! Stop! Security Division, Special Crimes."

Drover couldn't have been more shocked if he'd seen a dancing skeleton. His eyes bugged out and he screeched to a halt. "Oh my gosh! Hank? What...where...?"

"Drover, what on earth do you think you're doing?"

"Well, I...we were playing fetch. I'm chasing a ball."

"Oh yeah? You're chasing the wind, son. Eddy set you up and you fell for it like a duck out of water. He *pretended* to throw the ball to get rid of you."

"No, I'm sure..."

"Look at him!" I pointed toward the cake house. There stood Eddy, pitching the ball up in the air and chattering a wicked little laugh. We could hear him, even at a distance.

"Hee hee hee!"

Drover's eyes grew wide. "I don't get it. He's such a nice little guy, and he was teaching me how to fetch."

"He's a nice little crook, and he taught you how to make a fool of yourself. I can't believe you fell for it."

Drover started bawling, dropped to the ground, and began kicking all four legs. "Oh, I feel so dumb! I want to hide under the bed. Oh, the shame!"

I listened to him sniffle and moan, then gave him a pat. "That's enough. It could have happened to anyone."

He looked at me through his tears. "You never would have fallen for such a dumb trick."

My gaze drifted up to the stars. "You're right, of course, but it's too late to spill the mustard. We must move on with our lives. Actually, this might work out okay. You stalled him long enough for me to get here and put a stop to his mischief."

He stared at me. "Gosh, where were you?"

"Uh...I was called out on another assignment, but never mind. You go back to bed and work on your self-confidence. I'll get this mess wrapped up."

"Gosh, thanks, Hank, you're such a great guy."

"Yes, I know. Run along now."

He went hopping back to the office, as happy

as a little grasshopper. My gaze lingered on the little goof and, well, I felt a rush of warm feelings, the kind of satisfaction that comes when we're able to help a friend work through a personal crisis. Drover was ten bales short of a full load, but by George, the little guy tried, he really did.

Now, back to work. I marched forward and arrived at the cake house, just as Eddy was about to weasel his way into the barn.

"Eddy? Halt! Hands up and turn around, move it!"

He jumped at the sound of my voice, raised his paws, and turned around. "Oh hi. You're back. Find the ball?"

"As a matter of fact, I didn't find the ball, you little scrounge, because you didn't throw it."

He grinned and shrugged. "Yeah, I'm a rat."

"You're a rat, and a lot of other things too."

"What a rat. They ought to lock me up." He had lowered his hands and they were moving around in a blur of motion. "Want to see a trick?"

I marched over to him and stuck my nose in his face. "No, Eddy, I'm done with your tricks, and so are you."

Now get this. He reached his hand behind my ear and brought out a pellet of feed. "Bingo, magic, hee hee." He pitched the cube into his mouth and crunched it up. "Want some feed? Barn-full, good stuff. Share."

"Eddy, here's what we're fixing to do. Pay attention." He reached out and honked my nose. "Stop that! Eddy, there will be no feed cubes in your diet tonight, and you will not wreck my barn. You will disappear into the night and go find someone else to torment."

"Darn."

"And just in case you get any big ideas, I will be guarding the door."

A grin leaped across his mouth. "Might fall asleep."

"That could happen, but if you try to crawl over me, I will wake up and beat the everlasting snot out of you. Do you copy?"

His eyes darted around. "Want to play fetch?"

I gave him my Train Horns bark right in the face. BWONK! "Scram, Eddy, goodbye and don't come back."

Well, Train Horns got his attention. He scrambled away and monkey-walked out into the darkness of night, and finally I was rid of the little pest. Just in case he had any big ideas about coming back, I posted myself directly in front of the door.

Did I doze off? That is classified information,

117

but the bottom line is that Eddy didn't make it inside the barn, and when Slim showed up the next morning to load up some feed, he was pleased, proud, amazed, and impressed. He was so impressed, he gave me a special award: The Exalted Order of Beef Jerky With Oak Leaf Clusters.

Oh, and when Sally May heard the news, she saved the very best supper scraps for me that night. And who knows, she might have even called the newspaper and radio station and passed on the story. I mean, she was really proud of me.

Wow, it doesn't get any better on this outfit, and that's a good place to shut 'er down. This case is...

Oh, one last thing. Later that morning, I found myself standing at the yard gate, and heard myself say (this is a direct quote), I heard myself say, "Hey Pete? One last word. Thanks."

It hurt like crazy and it will never happen again.

This case is closed.

And don't you DARE tell anyone!

Have you read all of Hank's adventures?

And, be sure to check out the Audiobooks!

If you've never heard a *Hank the Cowdog* audiobook, you're missing out on a lot of fun! Each Hank book has also been recorded as an unabridged audiobook for the whole family to enjoy!

Praise for the Hank Audiobooks:

"It's about time the Lone Star State stopped hogging Hank the Cowdog, the hilarious adventure series about a crime solving ranch dog. Ostensibly for children, the audio renditions by author John R. Erickson are sure to build a cult following among adults as well." — *Parade Magazine*

"Full of regional humor . . . vocals are suitably poignant and ridiculous. A wonderful yarn." — *Booklist*

"For the detectin' and protectin' exploits of the canine Mike Hammer, hang Hank's name right up there with those of other anthropomorphic greats...But there's no sentimentality in Hank: he's just plain more rip-roaring fun than the others. Hank's misadventures as head of ranch security on a spread somewhere in the Texas Panhandle are marvelous situation comedy." — *School Library Journal*

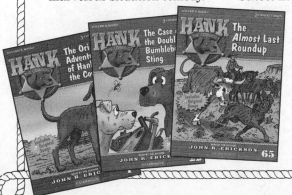

"Knee-slapping funny and gets kids reading."

— *Fort Worth Star Telegram*

The Ranch Life Learning Series

Want to learn more about ranching? Check out Hank's hilarious and educational new series, Ranch Life Learning, brought to you by Maverick Books and The National Ranching Heritage Center!

Saddle up for some fun as the same cast of characters you've come to know and love in the Hank the Cowdog series gives you a first-class introduction to life on a ranch! In these books, you'll learn things like: the difference between a ranch and a farm, how cows digest grass, what it takes to run a ranch as a successful business, how to take care of cattle throughout the various seasons, what the daily life of a working cowboy looks like, qualities to look for in a good horse, the many kinds of wild animals you might see if you spent a few days on Hank's ranch, and much, much more!

And, coming this fall: *Ranch Weather*. Learn about the tremendous impact different kinds of weather have on every aspect of ranching!

Love Hank's Hilarious Songs?

Hank the Cowdog's "Greatest Hits" albums bring together the music from the unabridged audiobooks you know and love! These wonderful collections of hilarious (and sometimes touching) songs are unmatched. Where else can you learn about coyote philosophy, buzzard lore, why your dog is protecting an old corncob, how bugs compare to hot dog buns, and much more!

And, be sure to visit Hank's "Music Page" on the official website to listen to some of the songs and download FREE Hank the Cowdog ringtones!

"Audio-Only" Stories

Ever wondered what those "Audio-Only" Stories in Hank's Official Store are all about?

The Audio-Only Stories are Hank the Cowdog adventures that have never been released as books. They are about half the length of a typical Hank book, and there are currently seven of them. They have run as serial stories in newspapers for years and are now available as audiobooks!

Teacher's Corner

Know a teacher who uses Hank in their classroom? You'll want to be sure they know about Hank's "Teacher's Corner"! Just click on the link on the homepage, and you'll find free teacher's aids, such as a printable map of Hank's ranch, a reading log, coloring pages, blog posts specifically for teachers and librarians, and much more!

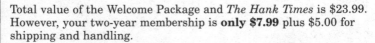

The following activities are samples from *The Hank Times*, the official newspaper of Hank's Security Force. Please do not write on these pages unless this is your book. And, even then, why not just find a scrap of paper?

"Photogenic" Memory Quiz

We all know that Hank has a "photogenic" memory—being aware of your surroundings is an important quality for a Head of Ranch Security. Now *you* can test your powers of observation.

How good is your memory? Look at the illustration on page 65 and try to remember as many things about it as possible. Then turn back to this page and see how many questions you can answer.

1. How many strands of barb wire are there on the fence? 1, 2, or 3?

2. Were there eggs on Slim's pants? Yes or No?

3. Was the Basket Upside Down or Rightside Up?

4. Was the Gate Open or Closed?

5. Which of Slim's knees was higher, HIS Left or Right?

6. How many of Hank's eyes could you see? 1, 2, 3 or all 4?

"Word Maker"

Try making up to twenty words from the letters in the names below. Use as many letters as possible, however, don't just add an "s" to a word you've already listed in order to have it count as another. Try to make up entirely new words for each line!

Then, count the total number of letters used in all of the words you made, and see how well you did using the Security Force Rankings below!

HANK AND ROY

_____	_____
_____	_____
_____	_____
_____	_____
_____	_____
_____	_____
_____	_____
_____	_____
_____	_____

55 - 61   You spend too much time with J.T. Cluck and the chickens.

62 - 65   You are showing some real Security Force potential.

66 - 69   You have earned a spot on our Ranch Security team.

70 +   Wow! You rank up there as a top-of-the-line cowdog.

"Rhyme Time"

What if Roy were to decide to give up his job as a feed truck dog and go in search of other work? What kinds of jobs could he find?

Make a rhyme using "Roy" that would relate to his new job possibilities.

Example: Roy grows beans to make this special kind of milk.
Answer: Roy **SOY.**

1. Roy becomes a full time scout leader.

2. Roy makes imitation birds to help hunters.

3. Roy joins the navy.

4. Roy opens a factory making fun things for kids to play with.

5. Roy teaches people how to be shy.

6. Roy opens a business that helps people find jobs.

7. Roy teaches people how to go around spreading happiness.

8. Roy starts a demolition business that knocks down buildings.

9. Roy takes over Pete's job and spends every day getting on Hank's nerves.

〜〜〜〜〜〜〜〜〜〜〜〜〜〜〜〜〜〜〜〜〜〜〜〜〜〜〜〜〜〜〜〜〜〜〜〜〜〜

Answers:

1. Roy BOY
2. Roy DECOY
3. Roy AHOY
4. Roy TOY
5. Roy COY
6. Roy EMPLOY
7. Roy JOY
8. Roy DESTROY
9. Roy ANNOY

Have you visited Hank's official website yet?

www.hankthecowdog.com

Don't miss out on exciting *Hank the Cowdog* games and activities, as well as up-to-date news about upcoming books in the series!

When you visit, you'll find:

- Hank's BLOG, which is the first place we announce upcoming books and new products!
- Hank's Official Shop, with tons of great *Hank the Cowdog* books, audiobooks, games, t-shirts, stuffed animals, mugs, bags, and more!
- Links to Hank's social media, whereby Hank sends out his "Cowdog Wisdom" to fans.
- A FREE, printable "Map of Hank's Ranch"!
- Hank's Music Page where you can listen to songs and even download FREE ringtones!
- A way to sign up for Hank's free email updates
- Sally May's "Ranch Roundup Recipes"!
- Printable & Colorable Greeting Cards for Holidays.

- Articles about Hank and author John R. Erickson in the news,

...AND MUCH, MUCH MORE!

HANK
THE COWDOG

BOOKS
The Collection

FAN ZONE
Fun & Games

AUTHOR
Meet the Creator

STORE
Books & More

Find Toys, Games, Books & More
at the Hank shop.

ANNOUNCING:
A sneak peek at Hank #66

Ever thought of having a Hank the Cowdog Themed Party?

Hank Plays Cupid:

GAMES
COME PLAY WITH HANK & PALS

BOOKS
BROWSE THE ENTIRE HANK CATALOG

FRIENDS
GET TO KNOW THE RANCH GANG

  Visit Hank's Facebook page

  Follow Hank on Twitter

  Watch Hank on YouTube

  Follow Hank on Pinterest

  Send Hank an Email

FROM THE BLOG

JAN 26 — Hank is Cupid in Disguise...

JAN 18 — The Valentine's Day Robbery! - a Snippet from the Story

DEC 04 — Getting SIGNED Hank the Cowdog books for Christmas!

OCT 14 — Education Association's lists of recommended books?

VISIT THE BLOG

Hank's Survey
We'd love to know what you think! GO

TEACHER'S CORNER
Download fun activity guides, discussion questions and more.

SALLY MAY'S RECIPES
 Discover delicious recipes from Sally May herself. GO

Hank's Music.
Free ringtones, music and more!

MORE

Official Shop
Find books, audio, toys and more!

LET'S GO

Join Hank's Security Force
Get the activity letter and other cool stuff.
JOIN
 SECURITY FORCE

Get the Latest
Keep up with Hank's news and promotions by signing up for our e-news.
Looking for The Hank Times fan club newsletter?

Enter your email address
SIGN UP

Hank in the News
Find out what the media is saying about Hank.
GO

FEATURED BOOK

The Christmas Turkey Disaster

Now Available!

Hank is in real trouble this time. L...

BUY   READ   LISTEN

HANK

BOOKS
Browse Titles
Buy Books
Audio Samples
Other Books

FAN ZONE
Games
Hank & Friends
Security Force
Educational Stuff

AUTHOR
John Erickson's Bio
Hank in the News
In Concert
Contact John

SHOP
The Books
Store
Get Help
Retailer Info

search the website GO

John R. Erickson,

a former cowboy, has written numerous books for both children and adults and is best known for his acclaimed *Hank the Cowdog* series. The *Hank* series began as a self-publishing venture in Erickson's garage in 1982 and has endured to become one of the nation's most popular series for children and families.

Through the eyes of Hank the Cowdog, a smelly, smart-aleck Head of Ranch Security, Erickson gives readers a glimpse into daily life on a cattle ranch in the West Texas Panhandle. His stories have won a number of awards, including the Audie, Oppenheimer, Wrangler, and Lamplighter Awards, and have been translated into Spanish, Danish, Farsi, and Chinese. In 2019, Erickson was inducted into the Texas Literary Hall of Fame. *USA Today* calls the *Hank the Cowdog* books "the best family entertainment in years." Erickson lives and works on his ranch in Perryton, Texas, with his family.

Nicolette G. Earley

was born and raised in the Texas Hill Country. She began working for Maverick Books in 2008, editing, designing new Hank the Cowdog books, and working with the artist who had put faces on all the characters: Gerald Holmes. When Holmes died in 2019, she discovered that she could reproduce his drawing style and auditioned for the job. She made her debut appearance in Book 75, illustrating new books in the series she read as a child. She and her husband, Keith, now live in coastal Mississippi.